BONE ISLAND MAGGIE

A BONE ISLAND MAGGIE MYSTERY
BOOK 1

The New Atlantian Library

Manhanset House
Shelter Island Hts., New York 11965-0342

bricktower@aol.com • absolutelyamazingebooks.com

Library of Congress Cataloging-in-Publication Data
Gregory, Peg.
Bone Island Maggie. A Bone Island Maggie Mystery, Book 1.
p. cm.

1. FICTION / Mystery & Detective / Women Sleuths.
2. FICTION / Mystery & Detective / Amateur Sleuth.
3. FICTION / Humorous / General
Fiction, I. Title.
ISBN: 978-0-692-51622-5, Trade Paper

November 2025

BONE ISLAND MAGGIE

A BONE ISLAND MAGGIE MYSTERY
BOOK 1

Peg Gregory

The New Atlantian Library

Habent Sua Fata Libelli

COMMENTS AND REVIEWS OF PEG'S BOOKS

Starfish

"Peg Gregory paints visual images of the settings that are so real I can almost smell the Sargasso weed washed up on the beaches . . . strong visual images both of her characters and of the locale, which in this novel comes to life as strongly as her people."

—*Writer's Digest*, **Cincinnati, Ohio**

"I just finished Starfish and I loved it . . . wonderful and touching love story brought tears to my eyes. Peg has a wonderful talent for evoking true emotion from the reader."

—**Alison McKinney, teacher, Houston, Texas**

And Then There Was One, a memoir

"A fascinating account of nursing in mid-century America . . . the extraordinary story of a remarkable, dedicated lady."

—**Joanna Brady, author** *The Woman at the Light*

"Veritably a bible of nursing history from 1955 until recent times . . . rich narrative."

—**C. S. Gilbert, Solares Hill, Key West Citizen,**

and author *Mother Poems*

DEDICATION

For Don and (posthumously) Ron, former members of the United States Navy Corps, and (posthumously) Larry, former member of the United States Marine Corps, all of whom I've always been very proud. With love forever, Sis.

This little tongue-in-cheek tale is also dedicated to former U.S. Marine Dennis Riley. Keep playing those pipes until the sun goes down, my friend, and never forget the good times with our Irish friend, Kelly, another good man who left this world too soon.

Other works by Peg Gregory

Starfish

And Then There Was One, A Memoir

The Bone Island Maggie Mystery Series

Bone Island Maggie, book one

Murder in Windsor Park, book two

The Trial of Maggie Metronia, book three

ONE

She got out of the Hummer and walked into the turnpike plaza like she owned the place. Although she was well over seventy, she still had the hourglass figure she'd been graced with since she was sixteen and a cheerleader at Key West High School. With the help of the bottle, her shoulder-length hair was still the color of wheat. Her eyes were such a light brown, they almost matched the hair. She had perfect vision since the cataracts came off, so wore no glasses except huge dark sunglasses that she fancied made her look like Raquel Welch.

Homer sat in the Hummer reading the sports page of the Citizen and smoking the stogies she'd smuggled out of Cuba. She brought some back for him every time she flew over from Cancun. He never knew what else she'd come back with and was almost afraid to pick her up at Miami International Airport for fear he'd be hustled off to jail with her. He flew or sailed to other places with her, but balked at going to Cuba. He told her he would go when the president lifted the embargo, and he could just fly ninety miles over from Key West.

She kept up with politics as much as he did, despite being as far to the left as he was to the right. She told him from what she'd been hearing, that might be sooner than he thought. He laughed and said, sure it will. He did not trust one word out of a Democrat's mouth and felt no differently about President Obama than he did any other liberal

1

bleeding-heart Democrat. Everyone should be conservative, like he was, and like every other Republican was. Now that the Republican Party had blended with the new Tea Party, it was even better. Taken over was more like it, Maggie reminded him.

Maggie tried to tell him the dad-blamed Tea Party was trying to destroy everything good and decent about America, every thing that had been done to keep the middle class out of poverty, and to help those already in the throes of poverty, but he just didn't get it. He'd understand when it hit him where he lived, she told him. Not wanting to keep the argument going, he conceded that maybe he would. She told him not to condescend to her, so he smiled and told her he was sorry, that he didn't mean to sound condescending. This ended the discussion and earned him another big smile. He knew she could never stay mad at him, charmer that he was.

He smiled when she walked back to the SUV with a ten-foot piece of snow-white toilet paper trailing from beneath her mini skirt. He knew better than to call it to her attention. You never called anything to Maggie Metronia's attention, if you knew what was good for you. And Homer sure knew what was good for him. Yes, sir, he sure did. He got any woman he wanted with that hunk of dough she paid him every week and he wasn't about to rock that boat. He admired Maggie because she was as eccentric as he could be, but he knew when to open his mouth. And now was not one of those times.

Without a word to him, she climbed up into the back seat as he held the door for her. She scooted over to the left side of the seat as she always did, and Homer drove out of the plaza and back onto the turnpike, heading south.

Maggie leaned back after fastening her seatbelt and watched the other cars as they sped past them. And, they all did because she made him go ten miles below the speed limit, irking all the tourists every time they reached the Overseas Highway in the Keys.

All the way down, traffic would back up on U.S.1 while Homer drove like a snail to satisfy her. Sometimes the other drivers behaved like fools and passed the Hummer, knowing there were cars or trucks coming the other way and they would barely make it back into their lane. When they came to the rare places with two southbound lanes instead of one, cars hurried into the other lane, shaking their fists, shooting Homer the bird and yelling obscenities at him for having slowed them down when they could have been in Key West hours ago, driving their usual eighty miles an hour. He'd just smile and let them vent to him, as Maggie rolled down her window and gave them all a good piece of her mind and shot a few birds of her own. None of them saw this coming from such a sweet looking old lady.

When Maggie opened her mouth, there was not an upper tooth in it, and the few lower teeth she had did not show. She'd refused to wear the beautiful dentures Dr. Troxel made for her up in Big Pine Key, calling them the most barbaric invention ever perpetrated on man or woman. The first time she tried to put them into her mouth the morning after she got home from his office, she gagged, threw up her breakfast and they fell out. She rinsed them off, grabbed the tube of Holdadent he gave her and squeezed a line of it all around the inside of the denture. She almost asphyxiated on it when it oozed out from the teeth and filled every available space in her mouth and throat.

She whisked the denture out of her mouth and threw it across the room, sending it flying out an open window. A rooster squawking outside the window wasted no time grabbing it. The last time anyone saw it, he was flying off down the middle of Whitehead Street with it sticking sideways out of his own mouth, with pink Holdadent oozing from it. A couple of scared tourists got out of his way and called the Key West Police Department to report that someone needed to pick up the miniature rabid dog with brown fur that looked like feathers, before he bit someone. Yeah, they said, he just flew around to Caroline Street. They assured them they would check it out. Instead they called Animal Control, who searched all day for it, without any success.

"Good riddance," Maggie said to her cockatoo, Minnie Pearl, when she cocked her white feathery head to one side. "I didn't want the durned old thing, anyway." That was the last time she had any upper teeth in her mouth.

When the dentist told her she still had good bone in her jaw and offered to put implants in so she could have non-removable teeth, she looked at him as though he just stepped off the nearest space ship.

"What?"

"I'm not about to let you put those things in my mouth. I know all about the microchips in those implants, young man. No CIA is gonna track me!" Her mother didn't raise any fools.

That was the last trip to the Big Pine dentist for her. She felt kind of bad about that, too, because she liked Dr. Troxel, bare feet and all. He had Lisa call her the next week to see whether she could convince her to come back to talk about it with him, but nothing doing. She wanted no part of it.

Granted, implants were expensive. She figured the government must not think old people needed teeth in their mouth, since Medicare and other insurance didn't pay a penny to help people afford them, but that was no problem for Maggie. It was the idea of the durned ol' CIA knowing where she was every minute of the day that got her. The money had nothing to do with it. She could have easily paid the thousands of dollars he charged for them, and she knew they'd look pretty. She could barely pay the mortgage in the rundown house she'd been stuck with after her parents died, but when she won one of the first Powerball lotteries when it came to Florida, she stuck the entire four hundred million, after IRS grabbed their share, into her regular checking account and never bothered to write anything in her check book from that day on.

She had Homer draw ten thousand in cash out of the bank every Monday, and that's what she lived on. She also had him draw five thousand more out every Friday morning. That was his weekly salary. If he kept the checkbook accurate, she never knew. Nor did she give a flying hoot. Her friends from high school pleaded with her to invest most of the money, or to at least put it into a good interest bearing savings account. Their pleas fell on deaf ears. Maggie didn't care if it was the Pope, himself, trying to convince her of something; if she did not see any reason to do it that was that.

Homer never said a word to her about it, despite several of them cornering him one day in Fausto's Food Palace soon after she won the jackpot, to try to persuade him to convince her she was living dangerously, having all that money so accessible to anyone who might be unscrupulous enough to try to get it from her. It was Maggie's business, not his or anyone else's, and he told them so.

They walked off in a huff. They never did like or trust that man, anyway. For all they knew, he was already stealing from their old friend. Heaven knows, none of them ever saw a penny of Maggie's windfall, even though she knew they were barely getting by in their three million dollar homes by the ocean, since their husbands left them for those young tarts. None of them worked to earn a living, and had to get by on what was left of their checking accounts, which by most people's standards was plenty, but they didn't see it that way.

Did she offer to give them the money to tide them over when they were getting low? Hell, no, she didn't. But then, what could one expect from someone who had been so dirt poor when they were all on the cheerleading squad, she could not even go for sodas after practice. Their memories were short on one thing. They did not offer to pay for them so she wouldn't feel left out. There was nothing wrong with Maggie's memory, and she sure never forgot that, to Homer's delight, when she told him about it. That was his main reason for disliking the vain broads, even though Maggie sloughed it off as though it hadn't mattered. He knew differently.

When they reached Card Sound Road in Florida City, Homer turned off U.S.1. Maggie never trusted that new section of the eighteen-mile stretch they'd taken ten years to complete. Never could tell when it would come crashing down, because everyone knew what inferior products road builders used these days. All the contractors cared about was pleasing the politicians who handed them the jobs. And that job was handed to them when the Republicans were in the White House. To her, that was enough said. Since he took office in 2009, President Obama was doing a great job of getting new roads and bridges built or repaired to put people back to work. But too much monkey business had gone on before he was elected; heaven only knew what underhanded tactics went on to get the builders to use those inferior products they probably used on that eighteen-mile stretch. She sure would never test them, no matter how much of a scenic route they'd created with the new stretch of highway.

That was okay with Homer who, unlike Maggie, did trust the contractors who built the new section of road and knew they wouldn't have dared to cut corners with all the eyes on them the whole ten years, but he enjoyed driving over Card Sound. It was one of the few pieces of Old Florida left as far as he was concerned. It even smelled natural like a place should, and he liked that earthy aroma. Maggie thought it just smelled like horse manure, but he told her no; it was the good smell of the earth. The state had tried for years to run off the squatters who lived along the bay in their run-down boats and lean-tos, but they were still there fighting off any developer who even looked like he was going to put up a piece of concrete. Rumor was they finally were going to be kicked off Card Sound in the near future, but they ignored it and went about their business as they always had, figuring the less said to each other about it the better.

Besides, Homer had yet to see his first panther on the seven miles of *panther crossing* so he hoped this evening would reveal one to his watchful eye. He knew his chances were slim, with only about a hundred of them surviving in the whole country. He still hoped he'd get lucky. Someone told him they came out at night, and he always tried to reach Card Sound right after the sun went down, but no go with Maggie. By the time they finished their errands on the mainland, she was always in a rush to get home, yet she insisted they stop and eat in Alabama Jack's. Before they reached Jack's, it was nearing dusk and despite looking hard on both sides of the road as they crept along, irritating those behind him, nary a panther in sight. He vowed to time it better next time, even if he had to fabricate car trouble to arrive in the dark. He *would* see his panther.

Concentrating so hard in his search, he hit a skunk taking too long to cross the road. Maggie threw a fit about the smell permeating the inside of the Hummer. Homer apologized only once, as always, when he did something to displease her. She smiled at him with her toothless mouth wide open and told him it was okay. He just needed to stop and pick up something in the Key Largo Winn Dixie to get rid of the odor, until he could get the SUV detailed the next morning. He grinned back at her through the rear view mirror, and assured her he would do that just as soon as they reached Largo.

Maggie never rode in the front seat with Homer. She liked him well enough, but it made her feel like she had a real chauffeur when he opened the door for her and helped her step up into the back seat and sit down. Besides, the other drivers who were shooting him birds couldn't see her return them, if she wasn't sitting on the driver's side of the Hummer behind him.

As was their habit, before they came to the dollar tollbooth on Card Sound, with its large, 'Welcome to Downtown Card Sound' sign, they stopped at Alabama Jack's for dinner. Jack's was really all downtown consisted of besides the guys who sold their fish along the road. She always insisted he come in and eat with her at the table she favored back in the corner beside the water. After he closed her car door, he hurried behind her so he could step on the long trail of white paper. He breathed a huge sigh of relief when it fell to the ground right before they got inside. She still had no idea it had been there. They attracted enough attention without toilet paper trailing behind her.

Homer was twenty years Maggie's junior and still a handsome man with his 'Semper Fi' silver crew cut. For over thirty years after he left the United States Marine Corps, and his antique business in Old Town after that, he played the bagpipes at Mallory Square. That's where he'd met Maggie when she was in her mid-forties and her long silky hair was not from a bottle. The best part was that she still had all her teeth. She had the most gorgeous smile he'd ever seen and always wore miniskirts and tank tops everywhere she went.

Maggie's biggest regret in life was the fact she could not call herself a Conch. Even though she moved to Key West with her parents and sixteen-year-old brother when she was six and felt as though she'd lived there all her life, she was not born there, so she was, technically, not a Conch. When she met the slender bagpiper with the easy-on-the-eyes legs below the Scottish kilt, she told him she was a Conch and he believed her. Then, when she smiled coyly and turned away, one of their mutual cop friends who *was* a true Conch told him a different story. In fact, it made him angry she would make such a claim. Homer convinced him to let her have her little fantasy if it meant that much to her. After all, what was the big deal? It wasn't as though one got a prize of some kind and was put into the Guinness Book of Records because he was born in the Keys and could call himself a Conch, was there? She overheard their conversation and that sealed the friendship for her.

When she hit the winning numbers on Powerball that night several months ago, she called Homer right away. He came over to the house, and they sat at her kitchen table discussing the future. Because he'd stood up for her all those years ago and was never ashamed to sit in a bar having a beer with her, even after she lost her teeth, she owed him. She never had children, though she tried marriage with five different men from five different countries including the U.S., before she gave up when she was sixty and kicked the last one out of her life. Her parents had died long ago and her older brother choked to death on his girlfriend's diaphragm last year when he was only eighty-one years old. That was before she won the lottery, so she had no one else but Homer.

"Why don't you come to work for me," she told him after their fifth beer.

He laughed and said, "I don't know how to do anything but play those pipes and sell your Cuban contraband, be it reluctantly. What on earth do you need me to do besides that?"

"I want you to drive my old Chevy and me into Miami tomorrow and get me one of those big Hummer things."

"I can do that, but that's not a job."

"I'm getting to that," she said after she took a big swig of her Corona. Looking him straight in the eyes, she said, "After we get the Hummer – and I want a bright purple one – I want you to be my full-time chauffeur."

After he finished choking on his Sam Adams, he said, "You want what?"

"You heard me. I want you to drive for me. I'm tired of driving myself and fed up with those crazy drunken tourists who almost hit me head-on every time I'm on U.S.1, so I'm going to stop it before I get myself killed. I'll pay you five thousand a week and throw in a nice big house on the beach up on Sugarloaf, like you said you'd always like to have. It will be in your name and you can do anything you want with it."

He was speechless. She always gave him a cut of her earnings from the Cuban antiques he sold for her and he knew she liked him as he did her. They understood each other's eccentricities. And she'd never slept with him. Homer respected a woman who could refuse him, stud that he was. She'd never tried to change him, either. Well, there was that one time he'd fancied himself in love with a gorgeous teenager from Argentina he'd met at Mallory Square one night. After a while he had come to agree with her – it was just too creepy for a fifty year old to even think about going out with a fifteen year old. Like she'd pointed out, it was just too close to being a child molester, even though the girl wanted to go out with him, too, and her mother had encouraged her. After all, as she told her daughter who looked twenty-five, not fifteen, he *was* a rich American, wasn't he?

This was before Maggie won Powerball, and he was barely scraping by between tips and CD sales. He did get a cut of the romance novels he sold for another friend, who also refused to sleep with him but books didn't sell very fast, so he didn't make much from that, either. But, other than that one little mid-life crisis with the fifteen year old, Maggie accepted him for himself. Homer appreciated that. But, to offer him such a high paying job and a home of his own, to boot? That was beyond anything he could have imagined.

But, a man would be stupid to refuse such an offer. And, Homer Wiley was not a stupid man. Before the tenth beer, he accepted her offer and took her to Miami the next morning where they bought a sparkling gold Hummer she liked better than the purple ones. On the way home, they stopped in a realtor's office and were driven around Sugarloaf Key to look at houses, until he spied one he fell in love with just twenty feet from the ocean. She paid the astonished realtor cash for it.

After that, she had the realtor ride with them into Key West where they looked for houses for her. She ended up buying one she'd always loved on Duval and United, an old historic three-story with wraparound porches and French doors. She also paid cash for that and Homer took her to see a contractor who got his crew in there the day after closing to see about restoring it for her. This, of course, was after he drove the sexy realtor home to test drive the big king-sized bed in his new house. Yeah, life was good.

Every day, without fail, Maggie rode her bright red tricycle over to the work site. More often than not, when she saw it, she changed her mind about something or other she wanted the contractor to do in the house. But, he, like Homer, was getting paid so much he just smiled and instructed his men to do it her way. In the end, Maggie had a beautiful gleaming white historic home with bright red Bahama shutters on all the windows and bright red trim around the French doors to match the trike she chained to the porch railing every night. The folks from HARC, who had to approve the changes since it was a historic house, could not stop gushing over it. It had become a beauty, after years of sitting there in a decrepit condition. The contractor had retained the authenticity of the magnificent historic Key West home.

Maybe Maggie was not a full-fledged Conch, but she sure felt like one now with that beautiful historic home a few feet from the Atlantic Ocean on Bone Island. This was a take on Isle of Bones, from the original name Cayo Hueso, the Spanish settlers' name for Key West. Every morning when she and Homer were not off to other parts of the world, she rode her trike along the sea surrounding her island and felt like the luckiest woman on earth to be living there. She smiled broadly to all the folks she passed every time she made that trip around the island. She would have felt better had she not lost all her teeth but that was a small matter, she'd told herself. She still would not allow that nice Dr. Troxel to put those CIA microchips into her mouth, no matter how she looked without teeth.

As she sat there staring at the boats on the water with Homer at Alabama Jack's, thinking about her beautiful home, she noticed something she had not seen before. She asked him for the miniature binoculars he carried in his pocket.

"Oh, shit!"

"What is it?" She rarely cursed, so he knew something serious was happening.

"Look over there in the mangroves. Isn't that a body lying over the limb of one of the trees?" She whispered this, not wanting to alert anyone else in the place.

"It sure as hell looks like it, doesn't it." He picked up his cell phone to call 911 and she grabbed it from him.

"What are you thinking? We can't call the cops."

"But, we have to report this. That's a human being lying there."

"Shush, keep your voice down. How would we feel if the cops came out, and it turned out to be just some old rags or something instead of a body?"

"But we can see it's a body."

"Well, I want to be a hundred percent sure before we involve anyone else in this."

"Oh no," he said under his breath, having no idea what she meant by the word *involve,* but knowing it was not going to be good, whatever it was. "Maybe I should call you Magnum instead of Maggie."

Frowning, she said, "I heard that." She swallowed the last of her iced tea and he called for the check. They left right away. When they got into the Hummer, she told him not to start the engine. She had to think. He sat very still, hoping she'd decide to let him call 911 and be done with it.

TWO

"Aw, Mag, we can't do that. What if someone sees us?"

"Don't be such a wimp and hand me that wet suit. It's too late to go diving in Bahia Honda like we planned, anyway. You can change in the front seat and don't peek at me while you're doing it!"

"You know I wouldn't do that. Sure as hell don't know how I'm going to squeeze into this thing in the car, if I ever do manage to get out of my clothes to do it."

Thinking he'd probably had plenty of experience doing just that in the car, she said, "Stop complaining and just get on with it before someone comes along and tries to peek in the windows. I know they're tinted, but if someone gets his eyes right up against the glass, he might be able to see through the tinting."

"Okay, I'm ready. Correct that – I'm dressed in the wet suit. I'll never be ready to do what you want us to do."

She was already out of the car. "I'm dressed, too, so let's sneak over to the edge and slip in before we're seen."

With that, she stepped into the water and disappeared beneath its surface. Not wanting her to get hurt, he followed suit, despite every sense in the world advising him against partaking in her outlandish plan.

The water was crystal clear with the sun still beaming down, so they could see their way clear to the mangroves. They had almost made it when Maggie said, "Look here. We can step up on this log and then right over into the grove."

Following her lead, her sidekick stepped up on it, too – right before it moved, and it wasn't because of the current. "My God, this isn't a log," shouted Homer. "It's a gator. Come on, let me have your hand so we can jump before his head comes up again, and he has us for dinner."

"Okay, I'm trying." Just as she reached his hand, the twelve foot alligator submerged like a submarine and then kicked right back to the surface with his tooth-filled mouth gaping for the kill. He caught her foot but her flipper came off in the cavernous opening, just as Homer jerked her to safety.

They fell back into the mangroves and were certain he still was going to make dinner of them, but he tired of the effort and swam off in the opposite direction. "That was way too close for comfort," an exhausted Homer told Maggie. "Now, just how do you expect us to get back to the car? We know there's at least one gator in there, and I'd bet my next paycheck he's got a horde of friends just waiting to get a stab at us as soon as our flippers – make that flipper, in your case – touch the surface of the bay."

"You worry entirely too much, my friend," she said, as she took off the lone flipper. "Come on, get out of yours so we can walk over to see that body."

"I'm trying. Don't go wandering off without me."

Just as the words left his mouth and she started to open hers in a retort, they heard, "Hold it right there, you two!"

"Oh no, look what you've done now," Homer told her under his breath.

"Not another word, young fella, or you'll be in more trouble than you already are. I've got 'em, Lieutenant," the robust officer yelled.

His lieutenant pulled his boat up beside his and the officer took his line to anchor it to a tough branch next to his own. Then, he held out his hand for the other man to take it, and they were both standing in front of the intruders.

"Well, what have we here," the Monroe County Sheriff's lieutenant said to no one in particular. "That sure looks like a dead body now, doesn't it."

"It sure does, chief. And, lucky for us that gator didn't catch his dinner, since we caught 'em red-handed."

"But, you've got it all wrong. We didn't . . ."

"Shut your mouth, ma'am, before I taze it shut for you!"

"Don't you dare touch a hair on her head!"

"Well, if you value this old bag so much, keep her quiet while we investigate what's happened here." The deputy looked at Homer with squinted eyes. "Though, I guess it won't be such a hard thing to do, seeing's how we caught you at it."

"But . . ."

"Didn't I tell you to keep her quiet? This is your last chance or you'll get it first, and then I'll take care of her."

"You wouldn't dare. She's just a harmless old woman," Homer told him.

Grinning at him, the deputy said, "Just watch me." He took the taser off his belt and the lieutenant grabbed his hand.

"No. There'll be no tasing. It's hard enough to maneuver over to the victim without struggling to bring her back if it kills her."

"Shucks, Spivey, what difference does it make if she's gone. She's a batty old thing. Prob'ly ain't never been right in the head."

"Be that as it may, we've got the cuffs on her now and she's not going anywhere. Come on – we need to check out that body before it gets dark."

Maggie and Homer, despite their hands being cuffed and in back of them, managed to follow behind them when they weren't paying attention, as they finagled their way through the thick branches of the mangrove's roots.

"Oh my God," they heard her say behind them. "It's Jackie Weener!"

"It's Jackie, all right."

"Damn it! Why in tarnation did you have to kill *him*? If you wanted to kill a mayor, why didn't you kill the one's in office now instead of him? Jackie never hurt a fly in his life. You could have done in McPatrick or any one of those guys sitting up there on that dais in Key West, if you wanted to do us all a favor – well, except maybe for Trixi. She's pretty cool and seems to be for the locals. And, most of the time, Clifton is, too, I suppose." His voice trailed off, but he was steaming mad at them and there was no question in his mind he'd found his killers.

"Officer, we told you we didn't kill anybody," Maggie said, before the tears started pouring down her cheeks. "We loved Jackie. Everybody did. We'd soon's shoot you instead of him."

"Listen to her, Lieutenant. She's telling you the truth. We didn't shoot him. He was a friend of ours. We wouldn't have hurt a hair on his head."

The deputy sneered. "It won't help to pretend you don't know how he was killed. You can't throw us off course. We know you stabbed him, and good heavens, man, you even cut off his toes! And, his hands! Geez, look at . . ."

"Okay, Mac, let it go. We've got to work this scene and get CSI out here before it gets dark. You two," he said, jerking a finger at Homer's chest, "you just stay put right there, before we accidentally shove you off into that gator's mouth. I see him hanging close to the boats, just waiting to get another grab at you."

"But, you've got to believe us."

"You'll have your chance to try to convince a jury, son. We're not interested in anything you have to say right now. When we get back to the station after they've come to cart poor Jackie away, you'll answer our questions. In the meanwhile, just shut the hell up and let us do our job."

Homer clammed up and motioned for Maggie not to say anything else. It was obvious the deputies were not going to believe anything they had to say. They would wait until they got back on solid ground, before they tried again to get them to listen to what happened.

"Oh God, I'm gonna be sick." With that, the deputy hung his head over the water and threw up. He lifted it back, just as the vigilant gator snapped at the contents of his stomach.

"Shit!" Lieutenant Spivey said as he saw what caused his deputy to vomit. On a root a couple of feet away from the corpse of former Key West Mayor Jackie Weener, was the bloody stump of his manhood with a bright yellow piece of lined paper on a twig next to it. The words,

'That'll teach you, sucker!' were printed in large letters, with a permanent red marker.

"Aw, man," Homer said behind him as he got a closer look at what was causing the commotion.

"I thought we told you to stay put over there," the shaky deputy said, whipping out his taser again, after he wiped his mouth. Before his supervisor could stop him, he aimed and started to shoot it toward Homer, who grabbed Maggie before it could reach him, causing both of them to slip and fall back into the water.

"Damn it, now look what you did. Hurry and help me or we won't have any suspects to question." He hurried to reach out a hand for Maggie, as his deputy, with great reluctance, did the same for Homer. He almost lost a hand in the process as the gator was there in a flash.

"Now, stay put and not another word, or I'll let my deputy use that trigger- finger and get you both with the taser. And, if he won't, I will. Then, we'll forget about hauling your asses into the station. We'll just hand you over to that hungry reptile out there and be done with it. I've had about enough of you both."

"She didn't do anything," Homer protested, risking the deputy's trigger finger again. The lieutenant glared at McElroy and he didn't release the taser from his belt, despite how badly he wanted to let it rip.

As they searched the small area of mangroves where the body lay grotesquely over the larger root, they were sticking a plain yellow post-it onto several roots as they came upon more evidence. The body parts were only the beginning. On one they found a topless tube of bright red lipstick that matched the red lettering on the note. On the next, actually taped to the root with masking tape, they found a bloody knife like they'd seen Weener use to get to the insides of his dead animals before stuffing them.

"Looks like he was done in with his own knife."

"I wouldn't doubt it." In a lower voice so the two suspects could not hear him, the lieutenant said, "Something's not right about this. Why would an old woman and a younger man kill Jackie in this way? Surely he wasn't having an affair with that woman. Unless – sure, that's it. Jackie must have been seeing the man's wife, the man gets the tube of lipstick from her purse, then followed him to wherever, and then, with the old woman standing watch, he does him."

"Sure sounds feasible to me. But, why her? Why wouldn't he want another man around just in case Jackie tries to run? Don't make sense, now that I think about it," McElroy said. "She wouldn't have been any help to him."

"Maybe she was his bait. Maybe, since they seem to know him pretty well, he was hiding behind something and she was standing out in the open. Then, when Jackie walks by, she strikes up a conversation with him. If she was a friend, he wouldn't think twice about passing the time of day with her."

"Yeah, and just as Jackie starts talking, zap, that one jumps out and starts brandishing the knife, she steps back and that's all she wrote. Jackie's stabbed in the back and they've got a stiff to deal with."

"Yeah, but it must have been hard for them to maneuver him up onto that root like that. I don't see any signs of a struggle here or even any blood trail - except that one." He pointed to the other side of the body and the deputy gingerly leaned over and saw what he was looking at. "Stay put," he told Deputy McElroy, "and I'll call Salute`. Until the tide comes in, they'll still be able to get some good pictures of everything and take some decent samples. We've got plenty to hang these two with and the crime scene boys will help us prove it."

He grinned at Homer and Maggie, who wanted to say plenty back to him, but she knew better than to open her mouth. She didn't know which would be worse, to be electrocuted or eaten alive by a twelve-foot gator, but she didn't want to find out.

It took only a few minutes for the crime scene team to get to them. "Shit, Mike, is that who I think it is?" Sargeant Chis Salute` and his two-man team gaped at the corpse upon getting out of the boat.

"Fraid so," Lieutenant Spivey told him. "We caught those two red-handed, just as that gator over there was about to put his napkin on and pick up his knife and fork."

"Hey, I know you," Sargeant Salute' said in an accusatory voice, "You're Homer Wiley, that bagpiper who used to play on the dock every night. Damn, man, you're a Marine like me. Why'd you go and do something like this? Jackie never hurt a flea."

"I di . . ."

"Shut the hell up, like I told you," Spivey said before Homer could protest his innocence again.

Homer glanced over at Maggie and her normally pinkish face was stark white. He felt worse for her by the minute. He could take their badgering until he got to call a lawyer, but they had no right to even so much as ask her one question. She looked so frail; he didn't think she would hold up to any amount of grueling interrogation. At that moment, she glanced at him and he managed a weak smile to encourage her to stay strong. She was so scared she couldn't even smile back at him, all her feistiness gone.

All of a sudden, something flashed in her eyes and she looked at him with the familiar gleam, as though that seemingly lost feistiness won out over her terror, and she gave him her big toothless smile, because she could see how worried he was about her. He breathed a sigh of relief. He knew as long as she could hold onto that feeling, she would get through whatever was in store for them.

"Okay, you two, let's get you in the boat. We aren't needed here, anymore," the chief of detectives told them, with one last look back at the bloody corpse of his old friend and poker buddy, Key West's beloved taxidermist, Jackie Weener, whom he knew had wanted just one more crack at being mayor before he died. He'd always said once wasn't enough for him to do what he'd wanted for the town. Now, they'd never see his smiling face up on that dais again. What a damned shame.

THREE

Maggie and Homer were taken to Stock Island and booked into the jail off College Road. It had been easier on Maggie than she'd anticipated. A female deputy, Nora Lopez, attended to everything. She didn't know Maggie except to wave at her as she rode her trike past her house on Thomas Street, but she empathized with her, believing in her heart of hearts that this elderly little eccentric woman could not have done what she was accused of doing.

As for Homer, her mouth flew open when she saw him in handcuffs. She'd had a few dates with him over the years, and though a bit too much for her, she knew he didn't have a hateful bone in his body. And, a person sure would have to have a lot of hate to do what the deputy said he was supposed to have done. She sighed, telling herself she wasn't going to get personally involved. All the same, she was glad another deputy was handling his booking.

Homer noticed Nora right away, and when her eyes met his, he shook his head "no" several times. She gulped and looked away quickly. She simply could not do this. She had a job to do. She never looked back at him.

"Okay, Ma'am, you're all set. I'll take you back to your cell."

For the first time, Maggie spoke. "Oh God, do I have to go in there. Really, I didn't do anything to Jackie. He was my friend, Deputy – Lopez," she said, squinting at the name on her uniform shirt.

"I'm sorry, it's standard procedure until your first appearance in court, Ma'am. You know – when it involves a homicide. Please, don't raise a fuss," her voice went down a notch. "It will go harder on you if you do. Just go into the cell, lie down and don't say anything to anyone. Trust me, I know what I'm talking about." She half-smiled at Maggie.

"All right, if you say so. I gotta tell you, though – I'm really scared. "Her lips quivered, but she kept the tears at bay. Until she heard the clink of the cell door as it closed and locked behind her. They fell, but were silent. She knew the young deputy's warning was meant to protect her from the likes of that deputy with the taser. Never in her wildest dreams would she have thought she'd end up like this. She almost smiled at the tiny slit they called a window, and thought she might have wanted to be thrown in jail, if she'd protested something as a young girl. She tried to psyche herself up to pretending that was all this was. She'd been down on Duval Street, protesting the cruelty to pelicans, and got arrested for unlawful assembly. It worked. In a few minutes her reddened eyes fluttered and closed, as Maggie went to sleep.

Homer, on the other hand, couldn't go to sleep. He was too worried about his friend who wouldn't hurt a spider if it ground its fangs down into her. Dear God, how on earth had he let himself get into this mess? He should have just called 911 from Alabama Jack's when he first saw the body Maggie whispered about, instead of closing the phone. They'd both be home in their comfortable beds instead of lying on bare hard mattresses in a smelly jail cell.

Nothing he could do about that now. He just had to figure out a way to get them out of there and out of the whole mess. The jailers took their time, but finally he was allowed to call his lawyer friend, Roy Haper. He agreed to come first thing in the morning. He was in the Bahamas and couldn't charter a plane until 7, so Homer would just have to bide his time until then. Though how he was going to do that, he had no idea. He couldn't even close his eyes and couldn't have gone to sleep, if his life depended upon it.

He didn't trust anyone in the S.O. and wished he could talk with his buddy, Tony, on the Key West police force. Tony would know what to do. They'd gone into the Marines together when they were kids, and

Tony had a good head on his shoulders. For a moment he entertained the idea of asking the guard to contact Tony for him, but nixed that idea as soon as it surfaced. The less he said to anyone in here the better off he'd be.

Despite wanting to maintain his vigilance, for Maggie's sake, sleep eventually overtook Homer's anxious mind and he remained asleep until he heard the wake-up call at 5:30. Sighing, he rose from his bunk and steeled himself to face the day. When Roy arrived, things would fall into place, and that moment couldn't come soon enough.

He almost asked the guard how Maggie was, but thought better of it. He'd stick to the plan and keep his mouth shut, while his eyes stayed open and his ears alert for any tidbit of news when they were all standing around doing nothing but watching him and the other few prisoners.

After breakfast, as meager as it was, one of the guards told him he had a visitor. He thanked him, as he followed him through the maze of doors to the room where Roy Haper waited, looking as fresh and dapper as someone who'd just been to the Bahamas.

"There you are. Sit down and we'll talk."

They shook hands and Homer said, "Thanks for coming so soon. I'm sure you had better things to do after your vacation."

The lawyer sighed, thinking of the little strawberry blonde from Sweden he'd left behind. Before he got Homer's call, he'd planned to extend his time in the islands for another week, so that he could continue his dalliance with her. But Homer was a good friend, as well as a paying client, so he had no choice but to charter the first plane out.

"No problem, pal. Now, tell me what happened to get you into this mess. And please don't tell me Maggie had anything to do with it."

"She has everything to do with it."

"Damn, I was afraid of that. Okay," he said, dragging his legal pad out of his briefcase and grabbing a pen that worked, "start from the beginning."

When Homer told him about Maggie's spotting the body in the mangroves, the gator, getting caught by the deputies, the lawyer couldn't

23

help himself. He started laughing, despite the pained look on his friend's face. "What's so funny?"

"Sorry, can't help it. Who but Mag would see a body in the thick branches of the mangroves? To be in her seventies, that woman has the eyes of an eagle." He chuckled again, and then waved Homer to continue his story.

"Well, that's disconcerting, to put it mildly," he said after Homer finished. "Never thought Jackie'd see that kind of an end to his life. Hard to believe. I know he used to play around a little, but I think he's been walking a straight line since Faye said she'd leave him if he continued on that track. Sure sounds like something a woman would do, though, doesn't it. Can't picture her committing such a deed, even if he had begun to stray again, which I don't believe he had."

"What can we do? I don't care so much about myself, but damn, I want Maggie out of this place. She doesn't deserve this and everyone knows it."

"Just hold on, pal. Let's get the first appearance out of the way. And, don't say a word unless the judge asks you something. We'll worry about Maggie, if they deny bond. And, of course, we'll plead not guilty."

"Do you think they'll arraign us both at the same time?"

"No, you'll be kept separated, but she'll have her first appearance this morning, too. Do you want me to handle her case?"

"Of course."

"All right, then. I'll go talk with her now, and I'll see you in the courtroom. Keep your mouth shut until then."

"Don't worry. I'm not going to do anything to get us in deeper. I want out of this as much as Mag does."

"See you in town then. And try not to worry. I'll get them to release Maggie this morning."

"Thanks, Roy." They shook hands again, and the guard stepped up and guided Homer out of the interview room.

FOUR

At 8:30 that morning, before either Homer or Maggie were taken from their cells, Key West Police Chief Lenny Doan had a call from his chief of detectives, Lieutenant Blake Butler. "Chief, you'd better get over here. This is real bad."

"I'll be right there. By the way, did you hear about Jackie?"

The burly detective gulped and said, "Yeah, that's why you need to come to the scene."

Puzzled, Chief Doan scratched his head and told Butler he was on his way. When he got to Duval Towers, he had to push his way to the elevators. What the hell's with all the press? "No comment," he told all of them who shoved microphones into his face, and hurried onto the car.

"What have you got? It must be something to have drawn those bloodhounds to the lobby this early." He smiled at the somber Butler, who led the way to the bedroom, without returning the smile or saying a word to his chief.

"My God! Looks like he bled out to every space in the room," he told him, as he grabbed his gloves and surgical boots before he stepped through the open doorway. There was blood spatter on two walls, puddles on the floor and it was difficult to see the victim for the blood on the bed. "Who is he, anyway? It is a he, right?"

"When you see what's under that sheet, you won't have to ask."

Doan gingerly pulled the sheet off the victim. It was saturated with still un-clotted bright red blood. Bile rose in his throat. "Just like Jackie," he managed to say.

"Yeah," Blake Butler said, in a husky whisper. "I hate to think what this means, Chief."

"Well, until we know who he is and whether there's a connection, we can't broadcast to those vultures in the lobby that we've probably got a serial killer in the Keys."

"The vic's Walter Stummond. Retired CEO of Strummond Steel in Detroit. Been down here for nine years, lived a quiet non-descript life. Divorced, no kids, and the ex is deceased, so no one to notify. Sad to end up like this, eh?"

"I'll say. You're absolutely certain of the next of kin situation?"

"We called Strummond Steel and HR confirmed his parents are gone and he had no siblings – not even a cousin that anyone knows of. His beneficiaries on the company life insurance are the workers of Strummond Steel."

"Nice of him to think of the employees in that way. How about his local friends or associates?"

"You know Jack Flatward. He was a drinking buddy, but said they never socialized outside of Don's Bar, and that was only once or twice a week. Strummond was a loner who seemed to like it that way."

"What about women?"

"Flatward said there was one woman he'd bring into Don's once in a while, but she had a heart attack and dropped dead a few years ago. He never saw him with anyone else after that."

"Who was the woman who died?"

Butler thumbed through his notes, frowning. He knew he got the name from Jack Flatward. "Oh, here it is. Polly Gayle. Lived over on Staples."

"Any chance she was married with a jealous husband?"

"That was my first thought, but Jack said no; her husband drowned in a boating accident about ten years ago. Strummond wasn't down here at that time. She never was seen with another man except him, and that didn't begin until three or four years after the spouse died." He shrugged. "Doesn't look like there's much to go on right now. Tony found a couple bloody handprints that weren't the *vic's*, but they aren't in the system."

"Did Flatward's story check out? Maybe he saw him more recently, they argued about something and this is the result."

"Sure, he was the only lead we had. We printed him right away. He's in the system, but it was a petty theft fifteen years ago; clean as a Thanksgiving drumstick ever since. Said it was a stupid thing to do, but he was out of work and hungry."

"You believe him?"

"Yeah, he's spotless."

The chief sighed. "I'm almost sorry to hear that, since it makes the other theory – well, no need to think about that now. Let's just see if we come up with anything the guys might have missed. Did you let Spivey know?"

"I called right before you got here. He said they had no other leads in Jackie's case, except the suspects they caught at the scene. And, we all know where they were when – when this happened. He's not even cold, yet."

"Has Spivey cut them loose, yet?"

"No, said he wants to talk to the State Attorney first. If Bonner says to drop before the first appearance, he'll let them go, but he said he wants to be on safe ground with this, in case we're all wrong about them."

"Well, hell, how can we be? They were behind bars when this went down. I understand his reticence, though. Something this bad, we'd better all do it by the book. God, I hope we're wrong, Blake. If we have a serial on our hands, I don't even want to think about the panic that's gonna hit the Keys from here to Miami!"

*

"You haven't been yourself since that awful murder in this building. Why don't you just put the condo up for sale and move back home with Daddy and me, where you'll be safe?"

Carolyn Cramer said nothing to her mother. She continued to hug herself and stare out the window at the people coming out of Cowboy

Bill's, a place she would not be caught dead in. She felt the same about most of the places on this island that others thought of as paradise. Why she moved here was beyond her. She just did not fit in with these people who seemed to have a dinner or party to celebrate any occasion or for no reason at all. Just look at what those friends of Patricia Monroe did when that publisher over on Whitehead brought her new poodle, Pascal, home from Miami. The man, who just happened to be the woman's ex-husband, threw a big party to welcome her dog to Key West! And, his wife sanctioned it, even though she had to be out of town. Can you imagine? Throwing a party to welcome a poodle to your town? A poodle belonging to your ex-wife? What some of these people did simply escaped her! And, some of those street parades. She would not even go *there* tonight.

Thinking about all this nonsense took her mind off what had happened and what she might know about it. She shuddered all of a sudden.

Margarite Sherwood stared at her daughter. Ever since she divorced that good for nothing Tim Cramer and left South Carolina to move to this place, she's been a different person. She was such a social butterfly when she was home in the Carolinas. Now she's practically a recluse. All she did was go to nonsense like those city commission meetings and meetings of HARC. Margarite had no idea what the acronym stood for, although she did not disapprove of them as she did those other people. At least, from what she understood, they dealt with keeping old historic buildings authentic. But the city commission meetings? How crude! Her family had never gotten involved with anything like city politics, except when they had to appear before them to get approval for their real estate projects, of course. All those elected officials had dirt on their hands. And some might even have blood on them, if the truth were known. Why on earth a daughter of hers went there week after week to listen to anything they had to say was beyond her. And now this murder right under her own roof. Was there no end to it? The sooner she convinced Carolyn to move back home and leave this den of iniquity, the better.

"Carolyn? Caro-lyn, have you heard one word I've said?"

The other woman turned from the French doors and looked at her aging silver-haired mother. She had learned at an early age to listen with half an ear to anything she had to say. The older Margarite got, the more of a nag she became. "Yes, Marga-rite, I heard everything you said."

"Oh Caro, please don't take that tone with me. And, how many times have I told you to respect me and call me Mother?"

Carolyn grinned and let her mother pout. She knew it was not a nice thing to do, but since she was a teenager, she'd delighted in pushing her mother's buttons. Calling her Margarite always was certain to elicit a negative response from her. And respect her? She never had. How could she when all she did was whine about everything? Carolyn never measured up to what she thought she should be, so what was the point of trying? And, since she got Tim out of her life, her mother was the only person she had left to belittle. It seemed Carolyn could not live if she had no one to put down once in a while. Oh, she was not fooling herself. She knew she had become a bitter middle-aged woman, but she just could not seem to keep the bitterness inside and be the nice genteel Southern lady she was taught to be by this meddling old woman.

God, how she disliked her sometimes. Patricia told her she was going to regret not trying to have a positive relationship with her mother. "When our mothers are gone, there's nothing we can do about the time and energy we've wasted avoiding a good relationship with them, Carolyn. It's a two-way street, and never the fault of just one party. You're no longer a child and you're hurting yourself as much as your mom when you act that way toward her."

Carolyn had resented that unsolicited advice from her acquaintance. She knew nothing about them. She couldn't really call her a friend. She was too much of a meddler, just like Margarite. Of course, she realized had she not poured out her feelings about her mother to the woman, she wouldn't know anything about their relationship, so she had only herself to blame for that. Did she wish she could love her mother, regardless of anything she did? Of course! She wasn't a monster. Sometimes it was an ache in her heart, but she never seemed able to do it.

Right now, she just wanted her to go home and leave her alone. She had always hated this town, after all. Carolyn wasn't so crazy about it, either. It used to be a nice place to visit. She actually enjoyed it at one time. That was why she moved here. Of course, she picked the wrong street to move to, after she made the decision to sell the house and buy a condo on the island. She thought living on Duval Street would be interesting, since she'd never spent much time here when she came down with Tim or even after they bought the house on Sugarloaf Key. Perhaps seeing it through her own eyes, spending time in the galleries and bookstore a block away from it, instead of the places he always insisted upon going, would put a different perspective on it for her.

Being on Sugarloaf had suited her just fine. Their big home was right on the ocean and it was peaceful. She'd never needed Key West as her husband had. It was Tim who raved about Duval with all its excitement. How he could go on about Sloppy Joe's and Hemingway, LaTeDa and 801, with those garish drag queens always standing outside on the sidewalk. Heaven only knew what they did inside the place. And, that time he got all dressed up in those leather shorts and open vest to parade around the street during Fantasy Fest. She was never so embarrassed.

And then there was Mallory Square, with its nonsense like that bagpiper walking around in his plaid kilt, with heaven only knows what's beneath it – if anything. Blowing on those awful ear-splitting things until she could just scream. She met him at a city commission meeting and he seemed nice, but come on – bagpipes? A kilt?

"Have you gone deaf? I asked you to move back home with Daddy and me."

"Mother dearest, I need for you to go to the phone and call Daddy to come pick you up. I have just gone through an ordeal and need to be alone. I have to think and I cannot do that with you pacing around my house like a worried Southern mother."

"But I *am* a mother, *your* mother. And 'Southern' or not, I am worried." Although she suppressed a sob, her voice trembled. "I'm worried sick about you. Wait a minute – what do you mean you have to think? Think about what? Oh dear God. You had nothing to do with that – that murder, did you?" Her hand went to her mouth as the horror of it sunk in.

Carolyn laughed and said, "No, I did not kill Walter Strummond. I never even knew him, except to say hello on the elevator. I have other things to think about aside from what happened upstairs. I do have a life." Maybe if you say that often enough, Carolyn, even you will start to believe it.

FIVE

"But I – I . . ."

"Please call Daddy and go home, Mother. Now. I really do need to be alone. I have things to do and I can't stand around here watching you wring your hands over me. I'm forty-two, not twelve. This is my home now, and I have no intention of moving back to South Carolina to run into Tim and his lovely new bride on every street corner." Actually, she could have cared less about her ex and his new wife. As far as she was concerned, they deserved each other. After all, meeting at Fantasy Fest? Her in nothing but bikini bottoms and body paint? Tim's eyes almost popped out of his head at the sight of her. He slipped her his card the minute Carolyn's head was turned, but she saw his reflection in her sunglasses. Well, Delilah was welcome to him. What kind of name is that anyway? She was probably a stripper. Just imagine – Tim Cramer with his own private stripper! She almost giggled at the thought, but restrained herself, so her mother would take her seriously about leaving.

"But, someone was just murdered in your condominium. You cannot presume to believe you are safe from this murderer. Why, I heard the police don't have a single clue about who might have done it." She fanned herself with a magazine she'd been thumbing through, even though the air conditioner was on and the house was a cool 75 degrees. "It might be someone you talk to every day – the doorman or the guard at the gate, even. A murderer can look just like – why, your own father or your pastor. Like they say about that awful disease, HIV. You can't tell by looking at a person. Or a rapist – why, I've heard they can be the most normal acting people around and . . ."

"Mother!"

"What?"

"Make that call or I'll do it for you." A begrudging "Please" followed the command.

"All right, I'll call Daddy and go, but please, be careful. Lock your door with both locks and don't let anyone in, even if you know him – or her. I suppose the killer could just as easily be a woman as a man."

After her father came to collect her mother, Carolyn did lock and bolt her door. She was more scared than she ever would have admitted to her anxious mother. When she wanted to tune her out, she could concentrate on other things. Nonsensical things about Key West and what she hated about the place, with all its eccentricity. But, when she was alone, that night came back as clear as though it just happened. She had no idea what she was going to do. She shivered again and wrapped her arms around herself, as she turned back to the window to stare at the life bustling beneath her on the street.

Last night, right before nine, Carolyn was on the elevator, bringing her small-wheeled cart up, loaded down with recyclable totes filled with groceries for the week. She knew she should not shop late at night, but it seemed to be the only time she could concentrate on something as mundane as her grocery list. Even though she did not like Key West and did not fit in, she kept busy going to meetings and even volunteered at the library. She did not want people to think her ignorant or aloof. She had to keep up on what was happening in the city. She would feel like a fool if at one of those rare dinner parties she attended, someone asked her about an issue on the minds of all Key Westers, as locals liked to think of themselves, and she had no idea what he was talking about.

As she was getting off the elevator, she was almost knocked down by that odd man with a thick beard and mustache. She could have been hurt if he'd bumped her any harder, yet he never so much as said *I'm sorry* or *excuse me*. His footsteps, as he ran down those metal steps, were so loud they still rang in her ears. She'd asked, time and again, for management to carpet the steps, but no, it would take a vote by the condo association.

When she asked the association president, Mike Card, when it would be coming up for a vote, he told her he'd put it on the agenda. Of course, he never did. Seemed like Key West subscribed to that stupid Jamaican "soon come" attitude. It even had its own theme song, written and sung by that singer she liked, despite not wanting to. He was such a nice guy, that Howard Livingston. He called it "Living on Key West Time." People here prided themselves on being different that way. Every time she drove ever-so-slightly above the posted speed limit, someone was sure to tell her to slow down, shouting, "It ain't the mainland, dammit!"

Carolyn gave her head a shake to stop drifting off-topic and get back on track. Still hearing the metallic echoes of his escape down those metal steps in her mind, she suspected why – when the elevator door was still open – he ran instead. Was she wrong to keep this information to herself? Then another thought crossed her mind; just as she'd seen his face, he'd seen hers. Maybe he'd figure out which unit was hers and she'd be next – if he really was the man who killed poor Walter Strummond. After all, there were only two units on each floor. All he had to do was knock on one door, and if the person wasn't her, he'd know for certain where she lived.

"No," she said, aloud. "That's nonsense. He's not going to risk coming back. I was right not to get involved." She'd told those detectives she knew nothing, had seen nothing and heard nothing. She couldn't just pick up the phone now and tell them she'd lied about it. They'd wonder why she kept it to herself. They might even say that made her an accessory after the fact.

No, she could not have seen the killer. He was just a man in a hurry to get to wherever he was going. For all she knew, he might have been visiting someone in the unit next to hers. After all, the murdered man did not even live on her floor.

*

Homer was startled to hear his cell door opening. He'd been staring out the slit of a window for an hour waiting for them to come to take him to the courthouse. "Come on, let's get you processed and outta here."

"Out – like released?"

"Come on, I ain't got time for no chit-chat. If I had my way, you'd be stayin'." He gave Homer a shove that almost knocked him off his feet, but he said nothing that would cause this joker to hit him, knowing he'd be up on an assault charge, if that happened.

He shut his mouth and walked ahead of the giant of a guard he knew would rather have a piece of him, than be leading him out to be discharged. He didn't know what happened, but Roy must have gotten the first appearance postponed and somehow, without even a hearing, gotten him out on bond. He would not ask, but hoped Maggie was free to go, too.

When he was handed his things, and changed into his own clothing, they gave him his watch and cell phone. The breath whooshed out of him when he saw Maggie in street clothes, waiting for him with apprehension on her face, not seeming to know whether her release was a good thing or bad.

When the two of them got outside, he gave her the biggest bear hug anyone had ever had, being careful not to hurt her. When he put her down, he started to ask, but then saw her big toothless smile and knew she was okay. Neither of them spoke.

Roy Haper was waiting for them when the guard opened the gate for them. "Hello, you two," he said with a big smile. "Bet you're glad to be out of there."

"What happened?"

"I'll tell you when we get to the IHOP. I haven't had breakfast, and I'm sure you could use a decent meal. It will be pretty empty of the breakfast crowd now so we'll have a better chance of talking things over than in Old Town. Come on; get in and we'll get out of here."

Over breakfast, he told them the good news – they were not out on bond. They'd been released because the SA dropped the charges. And, then he told them the bad news.

"Oh no, there's been another murder?"

"Yeah, I'm afraid so," he told her. "In fact, there've been two more. Only neither body was left in a mangrove this time. The second one was a trucker who made regular runs down the Keys with produce from Belle Glade. He got his throat slit" – he swallowed hard – "among other things, as he got out of his rig on Card Sound Road."

"That's horrible! What possible connection could he have had to Jackie? He wasn't in the food business." Homer stopped eating and looked like he was going to be sick.

"None whatsoever that anyone has learned. This whole thing's got law enforcement baffled."

Maggie raised her head and stared at the lawyer. "You said there were two since Jackie. Who was the other one?"

"Well, it was closer to home, I'm afraid. The *vic* lived in that upscale condo over on Duval across from Cowboy Bill's. Some bigwig rags to riches steel guy. And no connection, as far as anyone knows, to the other two."

"Isn't that where that nice woman who goes to all the commission meetings lives – Carolyn what's-her-name?" She'd gone back to eating, but didn't miss a word.

"Yes, Carolyn Cramer lives there," Homer told her.

Maggie looked at him. "Maybe we could . . ."

"Oh no, you don't. You can and will do nothing." Roy Haper could almost hear the wheels turning in that white head of hers. "As of right now, you know nothing about a murder – anyone's murder. Understand?"

"But what if we just . . ."

"Roy's right. We have to stay out of this now. We can't risk going back to jail."

She looked from one to the other and whispered, "OK."

Haper knew it took a lot for her to acquiesce to them. Maggie loved to be in on everything in town. They'd have to keep close tabs on her to keep her out of trouble. Gently, he told her, "Now, come on – relax and eat your eggs and pancakes."

She did as he asked, after a quick glance at Homer, who said nothing more on the subject. He loved that little woman, but they'd had a very close call yesterday, in more ways than one, starting with almost being Gator lunch. No matter what she wanted him to do about this second murder, he'd refuse to help her. If he had to take her to the Carolinas or somewhere else far from here and put her up in a hotel until all this blew over, he would. Maybe that wasn't such a bad idea, anyway. This whole thing was creeping him out, wondering who was next. He mentioned that aloud and Roy said it sounded like a great idea for Maggie, but not to do it right now because it would look too suspicious.

After they finished their breakfast, Roy drove them back to Maggie's, where his investigator had parked the Hummer after getting it out of impound. As Homer was backing the SUV out of her drive, he abruptly stopped and pulled back in.

He went into the house and called, "Hey, where are you?" when he didn't see her in the living room.

"Back here. I needed more coffee. What'd you forget?"

"Nothing, but something just occurred to me." He poured a cup for himself and sat at the table with her. "That guy who did Jackie in might have been hiding in those mangroves before the deputies got to us. He might have seen us, followed them and hung around College Road until he saw Roy drive away with us. I hate to say this, but he might be watching the house right now."

Her hand trembled so much she had to put the cup down. "Oh no, I never thought of that." Homer hid a grin behind his cup, as she said, "I don't know what to do."

He patted her shaking hand, and held it for a moment. "I do. You're coming home with me. I'll do some zigzagging on the way out of town, so he won't know which way we went, if he is out there watching."

"But I just got back. I hate to leave my home again."

"It'll just be for a little while until they catch the guy, and then I'll have you back before you know it."

With some trepidation, Maggie agreed, packed a light bag, and true to his word, Homer drove up and down several streets before getting onto U. S. 1, with her looking back through the side mirror constantly to see whether they were being followed. Now, he could relax, knowing there was no way she could get back to town.

After seeing her settled into one of the guestrooms looking out to the Atlantic, he went back to the kitchen to clear up the dishes from the light snapper dinner he'd cooked for them outside on the grill, after Maggie said she was going to bed.. He felt relaxed for the first time since they'd spotted poor Jackie's body. When he turned down the lights and went to his own room, sleep came quickly. He never awakened once during the night. And, never heard another word from Maggie. When he peeked into her room before turning in, she was already sound asleep.

Homer slept the sleep of the dead until after 9 the next morning. He smiled when he awaked and saw the glittering waters of the Atlantic through the slider. It was great to be home and it was going to be a good day. He showered, dressed in shorts and a tee shirt, and went into the kitchen to get a good breakfast started. He called to Maggie as he passed her door, telling her he'd have coffee and breakfast ready in fifteen minutes.

He was sitting at the table, already on his second cup of coffee, after his breakfast, when he looked at his watch. It had been twenty minutes since he'd called to her. "Maggie?" There was still no response from her. He hurried down the hall and opened her door. Her bed was made and she was nowhere in sight. He opened her slider and walked all the way around the house, but still no sign of her. He came back in and looked in every room in the place.

"Mag, I'm gonna kill you!"

SIX

Maggie had a hard time convincing the guard at the gate to let her om, but finally, after calling Carolyn to verify it was all right, he opened it for her.

At first, Carolyn was taken aback by the request to allow the woman access, but then Maggie might be just the diversion she needed. She's probably not even heard anything about the murders.

Despite expecting her imminent arrival, she almost dropped her coffee cup when she heard the knock on the door. When she looked out the peephole, only the tip of the petite woman's head was visible.

Putting on her brightest smile, she opened the door and said, "Maggie, what a wonderful surprise. Please – come in and join me for coffee."

"Thanks, I'd like that. I skipped out on Homer, so didn't get any coffee or breakfast, and I was afraid to go back home."

The hairs on the back of Carolyn's neck stood at attention like an Army battalion awaiting its orders. "Please, have a seat on the terrace with me." She pulled out a chair and Maggie sat, heavily. Although she'd gone to sleep almost as soon as her head hit the pillow at Homer's place, she'd awakened at three and that was the end of her good night's rest. As soon as the first light of morning came into her vision, even though the sun was not up, yet, and she was sure Homer was still asleep, she'd called a cab. From her house, she walked to lower Duval when it got close to 9 and the sun was bright in the morning sky.

After pouring a cup of coffee for her, Carolyn watched in silence as she doctored it. She pushed the tray of fresh scones and Danish toward her. "Please, help yourself."

"Thanks, I think I will. These look tasty."

As she watched the woman devour two of the scones, smothered in butter and jam, as though she hadn't eaten in a month, Carolyn feigned nonchalance as she probed. "Now, tell me what on earth you're doing staying out on Sugarloaf and why you're afraid to go home. You haven't had a break-in, have you?"

Smiling, Maggie took another big drink of the delicious coffee. She could trust Carolyn. After all, she attends the commission meetings. That said a lot about a person. "No, nothing like that. My home's fine."

"What then?"

"Well, I guess you know we spent night before last in jail."

"No! Whatever for?" She half-smiled, as she could see the pair getting into some kind of mischief. Seems Maggie was always doing something to keep things stirred up in Key West. It was worth going to those awful commission meetings just to hear her comments at the end of them. She spared none of the city commissioners, giving them verbal whippings, as though she were their irate mother or grandmother. None of them dared show her disrespect or interrupt her rants, either. She never needed to raise her voice to them. They always got her point and accepted it even though, more often than not, it was a denunciation of them.

"Well, you heard about Jackie's – murder in the mangroves off Alabama Jacks, right?"

"I – yes, that was horrible, but surely that's got nothing to do with you and Homer?"

"I'm afraid it does. We were the ones who found him. We were eating at Jack's when I happened to look over and thought I saw a body. We went back to the Hummer and got into wetsuits . . ."

"Oh my God, you're the couple who swam over to the mangroves and got caught by the deputies. Well, thank goodness they let you out on bond. Listen, if you need a good character witness, I'll be happy to . . ."

"No, no, we're not out on bond. They dropped the charges."

"Well, that's a relief. No one in his right mind would think either of you had anything to do with that ghastly murder."

"Oh, but they did. If they'd not found the other two – the one being right here in your building – while we were incarcerated, we'd still be in jail." She could not help but notice the sudden trembling of Carolyn's hands, as they tightened around her cup. "So, what can you tell me about that murder?"

"I – I don't know anything about it. Why would you think I did? I didn't even know the man. Saw him once in a while in the elevator, but that was the extent of my knowledge of him." She poured them more coffee, and drank hers down in one huge gulp.

"Okay, I'm not going to beat around the bush here. You and I both know that you do know something. You're shaking like a leaf." Smiling her toothless smile to reassure the other woman, she dunked a cheese Danish into her coffee, ate it all and then took another sip of the coffee. "Sorry – didn't realize I was so hungry."

"Glad you like them." Carolyn tried to return her smile, but didn't quite make it. Telling herself to brace up, she said, "That's absurd to think I know anything. If I'm shaking, it's probably just because I've never lived in a building where there's been a murder before."

"I'm sure it's unnerving for you. It's making me nervous, too, but no, you know something and if we work together, we can get to the bottom of it. I want to see the murderer caught just as much as you do. After all, he cost me a night in jail. Now, come on. I'm not leaving this terrace, until you talk." Actually, it was frightening for her to be out there, because she'd always had a fear of heights. She tried not to look down, although like someone driving by an accident scene, it was difficult to keep her eyes averted when she could see through the railings.

Carolyn stared at a couple going into Cowboy Bill's. The woman's waist-length curly hair was stark white, she was tanned and might have been a little overweight, but wore a tight leather mini-skirt, fancy cowgirl boots and a skimpy top loaded with fringe. She had to admit she looked good in the outfit. The man was even more deeply tanned with black wavy hair and Carolyn thought he was easily twenty years younger than his partner and as good looking as one of those country singers on TV. He was dressed in cut-off faded jeans, a leather vest with no shirt under it, and like the woman, he wore cowboy boots. All of a sudden he grabbed her and they started kissing right on that public street, behaving like teenagers without any common sense, completely free of either restraint or decorum. Carolyn sighed, half-wishing she had such nerve. Although she'd vowed never again to be taken in by the attention of a man, at that moment she wished she were somewhere, anywhere other than Key West, in love with someone who thought she was beautiful again and loved her so much he couldn't think straight.

"Carolyn?"

For a moment, she'd felt safe within her silence. "Oh, Maggie," she said, finally, surprised that it came out on a sob. Maggie reached over and put her hand over the other woman's for a moment, until Carolyn regained control. "You're right. I'm afraid I might know something and it's scaring me to death."

"You can't keep it inside or you'll be a wreck. Now, tell me what you know or think you know. Then, we'll figure out what we can do about it."

Carolyn unburdened herself to this kind older woman, who, even though she looked comical with no teeth in her mouth and was the most eccentric person she'd ever met, had a heart of gold. After she finished telling her about the man, she took a deep breath and exhaled slowly. Dear God, she'd missed having a real friend to talk with since she'd moved here. A friend who really cared what was happening to her and listened to what she had to say, without being judgmental. Maybe she wouldn't be so bitter if she'd had such a friend. Except for a little idle talk after the meetings, she and Maggie had never had a serious conversation until now.

"Oh boy, you have a right to be scared. If he wasn't the guy who did Mr. Strummond, then he must have seen something. I'm sure the police must have taken a description from you."

The other woman's hand went to her mouth and she feared she was going to start crying aloud at any moment. What was wrong with her? She'd never been a weak sniveling kind of woman. "I didn't tell them anything about him."

That didn't surprise her friend. "Okay, then, you have to try to draw him right now. After that, you and I can stake out this whole island, one street at a time. We'll find him, Carolyn. Don't you worry about that. Now, where's your paper and pen? I've seen some of your etchings hanging in Sheila's gallery on White, so I know you can draw him."

"I – I don't know about that stakeout business. I don't want to put you in danger, too. After all, he's seen me up close, and he'd be a fool not to try to get rid of me. If you and I are seen together, he might hurt you, too. He knows where I live, remember."

Maggie didn't skip a beat. "You're right and that's why you're not going to stay here. Come on. You can draw the guy after we get back to Homer's. Just pack a few things and we'll go. He has plenty of guest rooms in that big old place by the ocean. Trust me; he won't object. After all, I bought the place for him."

She smiled and Carolyn smiled with her, though she was taken aback at her last comment. Not one to gossip, but having heard such a rumor, she'd shrugged it off as none of her business. "I shouldn't, but to tell you the truth, it will be a relief to get away from here. I'll just be a minute."

~ ~ ~

"But, I have to get in there. It's a matter of life and death."

"Sorry, buddy, no can do. I have to respect the tenant's privacy."

Homer ran his hand through his silver crew cut. "Come on, just call Ms. Cramer, will ya? I'm sure she'll allow me to come up."

"You're as persistent as that little old woman I let up earlier. I'm sure you know her; the one with long light hair and no teeth in her mouth. She rides that bright red trike all over the island, though she walked here this morning."

His heart thudded, and he said, "Listen, mister, that's why I have to get into the condo. I'm the guardian for that little old woman and she's not well. She didn't even take her morning medications, and without them, she'll probably go into a coma or something. Actually, if you call the tenant, it will warn my ward and she'll take off again. Please?" Maggie didn't even take a vitamin, for the same reason she wouldn't let Dr. Troxel insert dental implants.

The man rubbed his hand over the stubble on his chin and pondered Homer's words. This used to be a nice cushy job before that murder. Now, seems like a man couldn't get a moment's peace. Against his best interests, because he knew he'd be in hot water if the boss found out about this, he motioned the man through without the tenant's approval as the gate rose above the Hummer.

"Maggie, I know you're in there! Carolyn, open this door. I have to see her."

His words were met with silence. He didn't actually see Maggie when he looked up at the terrace, but he saw part of Carolyn's back as she drank what he assumed was coffee, and she seemed to be motioning to someone. He knew they were both in there.

"Carolyn, I'm going to get the police to open this door, if you don't do it." Of course, he wouldn't call the police. There was too much of a risk they'd put Maggie right back into a cell. Chief Doan was a nice guy, but he might have a rogue cop on the force who'd love to see her back in jail. Him, too, for that matter.

After one more shout to them and pounding louder on the door, he turned away and left the building. They must have gone out the back exit, or he'd have seen them at the gate. He was heartsick as he drove through town without seeing either of them, or even the other woman's car on any of the streets. Going to Maggie's place bore no fruit, either.

Dammit, woman, what have you got yourself into, now? He felt that old familiar tingle running down his spine that said those two together were going to be trouble. He drove back to South Roosevelt and turned up U.S. 1. He threw his keys onto the hall console when he reached his home, and headed straight for the kitchen for another strong cup of her coffee he found first thing this morning, despite not finding her.

"What on earth!" There, sitting at the island sipping coffee, were Carolyn and Maggie, who was wearing her patented *who-me?* look that rivaled a stained-glass angel's.

"I brought us another guest – knew you wouldn't mind if Carolyn stayed with us a few days. She's kinda nervous. That condo murder, you know." She smiled at him and his anger melted.

"You gave me a real fright, dammit. I told you not to leave the house." Looking at Carolyn, he said, "Sorry, didn't mean to be inhospitable, but we've been through an ordeal for the past couple of days."

"I understand. Maggie told me the whole story. I'm sorry they treated the two of you like criminals. Anyone who knows you could see what a mistake that was." She smiled, but he could tell she was about as frightened as anyone could be. "I hope you won't mind my staying for a while."

"No – no, of course I don't mind. Maybe it will be easier to keep her here, having another woman to talk with."

Maggie grinned at him, not surprised he was giving in so easily. "Yes, that'll be nice, but that wasn't the only reason I asked Carolyn to come here. You see, the thing is – well, she might have run into the killer."

"Oh my – now what? Let me get another cup of Joe before I hear this." Whatever it was that Carolyn knew was going to land both Maggie and him right back in jail.

"Okay, tell me what you know. And, I'm not saying we're going to help you get out of whatever trouble you're in, but I'll listen." A fish jumped out of the water momentarily and made a noisy splash, startling the woman sitting across from him. He never noticed it before, but Carolyn Cramer was a very pretty woman. Her features were almost perfect, and that mouth. He blinked to take his mind off it.

Carolyn took another sip of coffee, found it to be too cool and stood to pour another for herself. She stared out at the pristine blue water for a moment, losing herself in the tranquility of it, until she heard, "I'm waiting."

"Oh, I'm sorry," she said, turning back toward him. "It's just so peaceful here. I used to live on Sugarloaf, you know. Right up the street from you, in fact." She sighed and then smiled at him. "I loved it here, away from all the goings-on in town."

As she sat down again, he said, "No, I didn't know that. I'm sorry you left. Do you still own your place?"

"No, my ex-husband wanted to sell it and move into town, so we put it on the market. It sold right before he latched onto – another woman. We split the profit and he married her. I went back to the Carolinas for a year or two, and then decided to come back here after he moved her back to the town we grew up in. It wasn't large enough for the both of us and that new wife of his. I just should have tried to buy another place here, instead of leaving. But since I hadn't lived on the island before, figured I might as well give it a try."

Homer smiled. "I'm glad you did. Otherwise, Mag and I would never have met you."

Maggie remained silent during this little tableau between the two of them, but she smiled to herself. She knew Homer was attracted to that pretty young woman. Maybe she will be his Waterloo.

Carolyn sighed. "Well, enough procrastination. I know you want to know how I figure into this strange crime we all seem to be on the fringe of, whether we want it or not."

"Maggie said you might have seen the killer?"

She struggled with the words, like something bitter on her tongue, and then spat it out. "Yes, I was coming upstairs with my groceries the night of the murder – of course, no one knew at that time there was a murder. When the elevator doors opened and I stepped out, I almost collided with a man running down the hall. After he'd run down the stairs, I wondered why on earth he was in such a hurry. Then, after the police came to my door to ask whether I'd seen or heard anything, even though poor Mr. Strummond didn't live on my floor, after they left, I started thinking I probably saw the killer. I was afraid to call them back, not knowing whether he would find out."

"Could you describe him to the police now?" He should just stand up, reach for the phone and call Lenny Doan. Get this out of his hands right now before she told him anything else. He knew from the way

Maggie was looking that going to the police was not what the two of them had in mind.

"Well, I could, but Maggie thought if I drew him – I dabble in sketching and painting – we'd sort of stake out the island and ..."

He glared at Maggie, looking again as innocent as an angel straight from heaven's door. "No! You're doing nothing of the sort. Don't you know how that would look to the police? We just got out of jail yesterday and I, for one, have no intention of going back."

"I'm sorry, but Maggie thought it would be a good idea."

"Listen, on second thought, I don't want you to tell me anything else, as I don't intend to be an assessory after the fact. I don't want to know what the guy looks like, what he said to you or anything else about your encounter with him." He ran his hand through his hair again, trying to figure out what he should do to get this out of his hands – out of his life.

"Look, I didn't mean to shout at you. This whole experience just has me a tad unnerved. You're welcome to stay here as long as you like. I've plenty of room and we'd enjoy your company. But, please, unless you're going to the police with what you told us, don't tell us anything else. And, for her sake and yours, don't let Mag persuade you to go through with that stakeout idea of hers. That's insane, and you'd both be asking for a lot more trouble than you could imagine."

Maggie didn't say a word, just glared at him. What did he know? She and Carolyn could find this killer if they put their minds to it. What would it hurt? They could leave Homer out of it, not even let him see the picture Carolyn was going to draw.

"You're right. I appreciate your hospitality. It'll be nice to be away from that building for a while." She heaved a big sigh, and then told him, "I promise I won't get in your way."

"I'm not concerned about that. I just don't want to see either of you – or me, for that matter – get into any more trouble over these murders. Let's all just try to relax and forget about it. Do you fish, Carolyn?"

"No, I never cared for it. My – I tried it once, and hated it. Hated handling those slimy little minnows or whatever the bait was, hated sitting out there in the boat for half a day, getting sunburned despite all the sunscreen I used, and most of all, I hated seeing those poor fish dangling helplessly on the end of that fishing rod."

For the first time in several days, Homer laughed, and told her he understood, but fishing was the second best thing he loved to do. Lord have mercy, how could a man think of sex with all that's happened to all of them since that first murder? On second thought, it was rather nice to have a man look at her like that again. It had been a long time. Still, she had enough to contend with, trying to hide from a cold-blooded killer. Not to mention worrying what the police would think if they knew she withheld that information from them. She looked down and took another long drink of coffee, as the man went out the door toward his boat, whistling as though he hadn't a care in the world.

"Okay, Carolyn, start drawing," Maggie said, after they watched his skiff pull away from the dock. She was surprised he'd leave them alone, but maybe he trusted Carolyn more than he did her, and figured she'd do what he said.

"But, Maggie . . ."

"You need to draw his face while it's still fresh in your mind. Then if you decide to go to the police with it, that's fine."

"I suppose you're right. It won't do any harm to get his image down on paper. As for going to the police, I'm still not convinced that's in my best interests. More than likely, they'd be suspicious of me and wonder why I withheld information like that."

"You didn't see any blood on the guy, did you?"

"No, but I didn't look that closely at him, either."

"You looked close enough to see he had a beard."

"Yes, I saw his face and then the back of him hurrying to the exit door."

"Okay."

"But I never noticed what he had on, except that it was all black. For that matter, I doubt it would have been easy to see blood on a black shirt and pants, even had I thought to look for it."

"Well then, for all they know, you hadn't put two and two together by the time they came to your door to question you."

"That's not a lie. I hadn't. Oh, okay, I'll draw him."

"Why don't you make a copy of it just in case? Homer has a copier in his den."

"I doubt we'd need two of them, but it wouldn't hurt, I suppose."

Maggie smiled at her. While Carolyn worked, she went to the pantry. "After you're through with that, let's take a drive up to Baby's Coffee and see whether they have any fresh cookies. They're the best around, if you've never tried them. Don't see any here, and Homer likes a few with a glass of milk before he turns in at night."

"Oh Maggie, I don't know about that."

"Oh come on, you know it's just a mile up the road," she said with a shrug of one shoulder.

"Yes, but – okay, I'm almost finished. Maybe by then, I'll be in the mood for more coffee and I'll treat you to a cappuccino."

Before they left, Maggie left a note for Homer, saying they'd run up to Baby's for some cookies and would have a cappuccino before they came home. Her face spread in a winning smile. He'd never be suspicious of that. They always had a cappuccino while the clerk rang up the cookies.

SEVEN

Maggie had Carolyn park her classic Lincoln convertible in the Mallory Square lot. Homer rarely went there since he stopped playing the pipes. It would leave them free to walk anywhere on the island they needed to go.

"I don't know why I let you talk me into this after we dropped off the coffee and cookies at Homer's. He's going to be so upset he'll probably kick me out of the house."

"No, he won't. He'll be worried, but that will be the extent of it. Now, empty everything else from your mind and concentrate on the faces of the folks walking around town. You're bound to see the man we're looking for, if you put your mind to it."

Carolyn sighed deeply. "Okay, you win, but what happens if I see him? Can't we just call the police and let them take over, as they should? You haven't told me anything except we need to stake out the island to try to find him."

"We'll see. We have to spot him first. Relax now, and sip your drink like a tourist on vacation." They were sitting by the window at Margaritaville. Maggie motioned to the waitress to refill their pina coladas. Carolyn didn't notice. She was staring at every man who passed by the window. No one looked familiar, except an obese city commissioner riding by on his scooter. His thighs were hanging over the seat, and a cigar dangled from his mouth. His young wife was going to be a rich widow soon, if he didn't lose that weight, as he was always saying he was going to do. With that thought she tried to concentrate upon what her friend was saying.

Maggie knew her small talk wasn't helping that much, but she didn't know what else to do. Carolyn's nerves were taut as a violin's strings as she watched for the man who'd almost run her down the day of the murder. "Did I ever tell you what happened the day I threw my dentures out the window?"

"Wh – what did you say, Mag?"

She repeated it, and finally got a smile from her. "It was the funniest thing you ever saw. Here was this rooster, who'd been getting on my nerves for an hour, just standing outside my window. When I threw the danged dentures out, he wasted no time grabbing them in his mouth and the Holdadent foam made him look like a rabid dog. I was too mad at the time to laugh, but the more I thought of it, the funnier it was. I could just imagine what people thought when they saw him scurrying down Whitehead like a miniature mad dog with this pink foam coming from its mouth."

Carolyn visibly relaxed and laughed at the thought of the foaming rooster hurrying down the street. "Now, that's a funny story." She tilted her head at the older woman whose smile was fixed on her face. She appreciated what she was trying to do. "Seriously, did you never consider asking your dentist to put implants in your mouth, so you could have permanent teeth again? It would give you back your beautiful smile. I hear they do a good job and you can't tell they're not your real teeth, Maggie."

Leaning closer, the older woman said, "Yes, I thought about it. In fact, that nice Dr. Troxel suggested doing it for me."

"He's my dentist, too, and he does great work. So, why didn't you let him do it?"

Continuing to lean across the table so no one else would hear, Maggie told her, "It would have been nice to have teeth again. I miss my smile, but with those microchips in each implant, I just couldn't take the risk. Who knows who might have been able to get to me with those?"

Carolyn's eyes widened and her mouth flew open. Microchips? She knew Maggie was eccentric, but that was beyond peculiar, and she couldn't suppress a laugh. "Where did you hear such a thing? They don't put microchips in dental implants."

"No one told me about them. I just know things. The CIA knows enough about all of us, what with that list Cheney started when he and Bush were in office. We don't need to give them more ammunition. It's too easy for them to find us with microchips in our mouths."

Swallowing a giggle, Carolyn told her, "You're not a criminal and neither am I. What would the CIA want with either of us?"

"Just mark my words, my friend, and stay vigilant. After all, you attend the city meetings, too, and God knows how outspoken I am at them. One day out of the blue they'll knock on your door and take you to Gitmo, lock you up and throw away the key."

The giggle came out. "Oh Maggie, you're such a delight. I'm not worried about being locked away on Guatanamo Bay or anywhere else by the CIA. I'm not a wanted fugitive or a big protester, so . . ." Her hand flew to her mouth. "There he is!"

"Where? What's he wearing?"

"He's still in black – shorts this time – and has a baseball cap on backwards. There," she pointed, "he's turning onto Fleming."

Maggie reached in her pockets, drew out a number of bills, without looking at them, and threw them on the table. She'd left the waitress three hundred dollars for two coffees. "Come on, let's go."

As they hurried out the door, the smiling waitress called, "Thank you!" She'd had large tips before, but never anything like this for a couple cups of coffee. It will pay her share of the rent for the month. She got her friend, Karen, to cover her tables, took an early break and hurried out the door to pay Jeremy, who worked at a B and B down Duval. He was shocked she had it this soon. She usually had to pay him later in the month. "Just take it before I change my mind and buy that dress I've been drooling over all week," Suzy told him, the smile still spreading on her young tanned face.

Her benefactors walked as fast as they could, but couldn't keep up with the man in black. He kept his head down toward the sidewalk, as he hurried up Fleming Street. They watched as he turned into the parking lot of Fausto's market, and ducked behind the grocery store. "Now what? I don't think we'd better walk behind the store, Maggie. We'd be trapped in there with him and he's probably got a weapon."

"You're right. Let's go to the other side of the store and see where he goes when he comes out." They almost ran across the parking lot to get to the other side, when they heard the engine of a vehicle gaining on them.

"In!" Homer stopped right in front of them, his tires squealing. "I saw him, too, and if he sees either of you chasing him, he's going to hurt you if he's the killer. Come on – get in. Now!"

The two women got into the Hummer, with reluctance, and Homer pulled over into a parking place on the other side of the store. "What in hell were you thinking? Are you trying to get yourselves killed? Why didn't you just call the police when you saw him? They could have had him in a flash."

Maggie bit her lip, and looked at Carolyn, wedged between the two of them. She didn't say a word, and neither did the other woman, who couldn't bring herself to look at their rescuer.

"Well, you don't have to worry; I called them." The sirens got louder, as they sat there. They couldn't see behind the store, but hoped he was still there.

"Homer, let's get out of here, then. Carolyn doesn't want them to know she withheld information from them."

"Yes, please, let's go," Carolyn told him. "I don't think I can face the police right now."

"Sorry, ladies, I told them I'd wait for them here. Dammit – there he goes. I – and here's the cops."

Both women wanted to shrink down to nothing when they saw the uniforms approaching from both sides. They were in for a peck of trouble and Maggie, for one, did not want to see the inside of a jail again.

"Okay, where'd he go? No one's behind Fausto's."

"I know," Homer told him. "We just saw him running up Bahama. He's about six-two, sorta stocky build, full beard, dressed in black shorts and shirt, with a backwards black baseball cap."

The detective radioed the information to the policemen who'd answered the call from Homer. "Okay, I want the three of you to follow me to the station."

Maggie blanched. Her "Oh no," was so low that the detective asked her to repeat it. She smiled and said, "Let's go."

As they turned back onto Duval from the side street, Homer said, "Unless they put us into separate interview rooms, let me do the talking."

"I appreciate that, but it's time I told them exactly what happened on the night of the murder. You and Maggie don't need to risk going back to jail on my account."

He smiled and patted her knee. "No, Carolyn, we're all in this together. We're not going to leave you in a lurch. Don't worry. It's gonna be okay."

"I still don't think you two should get involved."

"But, we are involved," Maggie told her. "No one's taking the rap for anything." Her Ma Barker elicited a grin from Homer.

"All the same, I'm going to tell them everything."

"That's my girl." Homer patted her knee again. "You'll see it'll go well for you. We'll back you up on it." Maggie nodded her head and smiled at Carolyn.

Carolyn bit the corner of her lower lip so hard she drew blood. She ran her tongue over the spot. Homer saw this, and emitted a small groan under his breath, which neither woman heard. "I hope you're right. But what if they don't catch the guy? Surely he saw Mag and I walking fast toward him. What if he comes after us?"

"Let's not worry about the what-ifs. We're gonna take it one minute at a time and we'll get through this. Besides, he'd have to go through this Marine to get to you and if he did that, he'd live to regret it."

His smile was reassuring and she tried to relax. They passed Bayview Park and the pond with its dinosaur sculpture floating among the gentle ripples, as they turned into the police station parking lot moments later.

Carolyn loved the weeks when the artists and sculptors placed their creations throughout the island. One never knew what she'd see around town that week, or where they'd turn up. The dinosaur was, by far, her favorite, looking for all the world like he belonged right there.

The detective was waiting at the door of his car when they pulled into the parking lot behind him. It dawned on Homer that he surely didn't see them as suspects, or they'd have been in the back of his car in handcuffs, instead of being allowed to drive behind the cop. He didn't say this to Maggie or Carolyn. He wanted them to sweat so they'd stay put the next time. A look of understanding passed between the officer and him.

EIGHT

"Okay, you can forget about trying to lie your way out of this. I know the three of you know something about this murder and I intend to find out what it is."

Surprised to find themselves all in the same interview room, none of the three said a word. Homer glanced at the two women. Carolyn looked frightened as a deer caught in the headlights, a pretty little doe, at that. Maggie didn't look much better.

"Let's start with you. You look like you know a hell of a lot about this case. Do you?" His look was menacing to the woman who'd begun to tremble, despite trying with all her might to stay calm, as Homer told them to do. "I'm waiting, Ms. Cramer."

She looked at Maggie, then her head swiveled toward Homer, who smiled his encouragement. Her deep breath was the only sound in the room. The detective waited for her to speak. "Look," he said, "you aren't a suspect. We just want to know what you know about that day. That's all." This time he honored her with an almost-smile.

"Well, I – I really don't know much."

"Let us be the judge of that, Ma-am." He tapped the table with a ruler he found in the center. The sound was grating on her already fragile nervous system.

"All right." She drew in another deep breath and exhaled slowly, as the tapping stopped. "I'd gone to Fausto's that night. I was getting out

59

of the elevator with my cart full of groceries. All of a sudden, out of nowhere, this man ran past me, nearly knocking me down. Some of my apples fell out of the tote bags, so I stooped to pick them up and didn't look at him again. I noticed he had a beard and was dressed in black. That's all I saw of him and then I heard him open the exit door and take the stairs. That did strike me as odd, when he could have just used the elevator. After all, its doors were standing wide open. That's it, Sargeant."

"Lieutenant," he corrected. "Lieutenant Butler."

"I – yes, Lieutenant."

"Why didn't you tell us this when we questioned you the day of the murder?"

"I – it didn't occur to me the two things might be related until after you left."

"Are you sure you weren't trying to protect him, giving him time to get out of town, or at least, find a quick place to hide? Maybe he was under your bed when we came to your door."

"Look, stop badgering her like she did something wrong."

"And you stay the hell out of it. I'm not talking to you. If you want, we can move you to a room by yourself, until we get around to you." His old friend glared at him, and Homer backed down with both hands in front of him in surrender mode.

"That's more like it" Turning back toward Carolyn, he said, "Now, think very carefully. Did you see enough of his face to work with one of our men, so we can get a drawing out there?"

Carolyn reached into her pocket and the detective's hand automatically went to his holster. He relaxed when she pulled out the drawing she'd made earlier. The detective's eyebrows rose. "This is good. We'll make copies of it and get it to all the officers in town. I'll fax it over to the S.O., since they're working Jackie's case and that poor trucker's."

She blew out a breath and her whole face relaxed. "Can we go now - please?"

Butler looked at her for a long moment. "Sure. You can leave, but from now on you're not to play cops and robbers. We'll take it from here. Got that?" His eyes glared at each of them.

Homer spoke for them. "Yes, we'll do as you say and stay out of it. Come on, ladies."

"Not so fast. I still want to talk with the two of you. Explain to me why, when you were let go from Jackie's case, you're involved to your kneecaps in this one? Surely, you didn't like jail that much."

"We aren't involved with this one. We just wanted to help a friend. That's all." Maggie's voice was weak and she sounded frightened.

He glared at her. Finally, he said, "Well, the next time you want to help a friend, you'd better be damned sure he or she isn't involved in a crime in some way or you'll definitely be hauled back into lockup!"

"We hear you, Detective. Now, can I get these ladies home?"

"Yeah, but we'll want to speak with Ms. Cramer again, so don't even think of taking them out of town."

"They'll be staying on Sugarloaf with me, so you don't have to worry about that."

"Okay – get out of here, before I change my mind," he told them with a swipe of his hand, grinning from ear to ear as soon as they were out of sight. Homer, you sure can pick 'em. When Bob Short walked into the hallway behind him, his grin had grown to full-blown laughter.

"What's so funny?"

"Just thinking how easily Homer can get himself wrapped up in trouble."

"You got that right."

"That Cramer woman is sure a looker, isn't she."

"Save your breath, Loo. She won't go out with anyone. Trust me, I've tried."

His boss looked at him with a wry smile, laughed again, clapped him on the back, and said, "Let's get outta here and help the guys catch this killer, if that's what he is."

~ ~ ~

"Where's your car?"

"Over at Mallory Square."

"Should have known that's where Mag would tell you to hide it," Homer said with a grin.

"She thought that'd be the last place you'd think to look." She returned his smile, but he could tell she was still shaken from the paleness surrounding her pink lips.

On the way home Maggie was quiet. Too quiet. Breaking the silence, Homer said, "You aren't saying anything. I think that trip to headquarters bothered you more than you thought it would."

"It didn't feel good. If I never see the inside of that place or the sheriff's office, again, I'll be happy. I have to tell you, I was shaking in my boots. I just knew they were gonna throw us back in the slammer."

He grinned again at the language she'd developed since this whole thing began over on Card Sound. "Yeah, we sure don't want to go back there."

They waited in his driveway for Carolyn to arrive behind them. When she did, Homer opened her door and helped her out. He wasn't surprised to see she was still shaking. "Come on, let's go in and have a hot cup of coffee and some of Baby's cookies." She smiled at him, but like Maggie, was saying nothing.

"You okay?"

"Sure. Just a little spooked by the police station, I suppose." She threw an arm around the little woman and they walked into Homer's beach house. She breathed a sigh of relief to be there, knowing deep in her heart that she could never go back to that condo to live.

As they sat in the airy kitchen having their coffee and snack, she said, "Do either of you know a realtor who would list my place without my going back there?"

Homer looked surprised. "Are you sure you want to do that? I mean, I'm no shrink, but I still think now isn't the time to make such a big decision, Carolyn. You're going to feel better about everything once this is all over."

"No, I don't want to go back to the island to live. I'm sure of that. I always hated living on Duval to begin with, and now, there's even more reason to get out of there. It's just not for me."

Not wanting to help her make a mistake, neither Homer nor Maggie offered the name of a realtor. "I suppose I could call the one who sold my house," she said, mostly to herself.

She looked around her at his sink counter, the fish scales and blood that were still there. He'd thrown the fish into the fridge before he took off to hunt for them. He saw her taking it in, but said nothing.

After a while, he looked at Maggie, who was still pale. "Why don't you make us another pot of Joe while I finish cleaning these fish? I'll put them on the grill, so we can eat dinner early, since none of us had lunch."

She perked up with something to do and told Carolyn to sit there and relax. "We'll take care of everything."

"Thanks, I appreciate that. To tell the truth, I feel like my legs wouldn't hold me up if I tried to get out of this chair. Don't know why I'm still so shaky."

"Hey, you said you'd never been inside a police station, much less been interrogated by the cops. Who wouldn't be affected by that?" He'd paused on his way outside when he heard her say that.

"I suppose you're right. I hope it'll be my last time, too." She smiled, but it didn't reach her eyes.

"Look, hon, we won't be insulted if you go in and lie down for awhile. You've had a bad experience, starting with seeing that guy the night of the murder. You don't have to stay in here making idle conversation with us."

"Homer's right. Go on now and have a little rest. We'll call you when dinner's ready."

"You've both been so kind to me the past several hours. I've lived down here for quite a while now, but except for the two of you, I can't really say I have any friends in the Keys."

Homer washed his hands, wiped them on a dishtowel and went to her. He took her by the hand and she stood, allowing him to walk with her back to her room. "Just kick off your sandals and lie down. I'll put this afghan over you and maybe you'll go to sleep. I'm in no hurry to get the fish on the grill. Maggie's already starting potatoes and veggies, and I'll throw the fish on the grill when that's ready, so it'll be a while."

"Thanks." She gave him a big smile. "I've never seen this side of you. It's nice to know it exists."

Tucking the afghan around her, he leaned over and buzzed her lips with his own. "Just don't spread that rumor around the island," he said, with a small laugh.

She caught his hand as he was turning to go back into the kitchen. "Seriously, I want to thank you for everything you're doing for me. You haven't even given me a deadline for getting out of your home."

The smile she gave him that time was a thousand watts of sweetness, and it was all the man could do not to lie down on that bed with her and make such love to her she'd never forget it. He swallowed the lump in his throat and turned away from her. "I just want you to feel better. Have a good rest." He went out the door, closing it behind him, wondering why this woman affected him differently than most of the other women he'd had no qualms about bedding. Then, he told himself to forget it. Now, and maybe never, was not the time to entertain thoughts of a relationship with her, so he wouldn't even muddy the already thick waters by trying. They all had enough on their minds with these ghastly murders.

NINE

To Carolyn's surprise, they'd no sooner finished breakfast the following morning, when Lt. Butler and Sgt. Short appeared on Homer's doorstep, asking for her.

"What the – we answered all your questions yesterday. What are you doing here now?"

"We need to speak with Ms. Cramer again. She *is* here, isn't she?"

"No, I put her on a flight to Brazil last night."

"You what!" The lieutenant's face was scarlet.

"Of course, she's here. We told you she'd stay put here, didn't we."

At that moment, Maggie and Carolyn appeared from the back deck. "You wanted to see me?"

"Yes, if you don't mind. We have a few more questions. We can ask them here, if you'd like." Honey dripped from his voice, but he didn't fool her. She knew she was a suspect, despite his saying she wasn't.

"Of course you can question her here, damn it. She's not going back to headquarters."

"I asked the lady."

"It'll be okay." Her smile belied her true state, but it was enough to quiet the man. He motioned the officers into the kitchen. Maggie produced cups of coffee, which they accepted eagerly, with the donuts she'd put on a plate.

"Thanks," they said in unison, as each took a donut. They'd been out all night searching for the suspect, and hadn't stopped for breakfast this morning. Butler took a gulp of the coffee, before he spoke again.

"Now, I'd like to go over your answers from yesterday." He glanced at Homer who was glaring at him. If looks could kill, even though he'd been in lock-up during the last couple of murders, he'd say Homer was his real suspect.

"Of course. Anything."

"For starters, tell me how you met the suspect."

"I told you I never met him. He just ran into me."

As though she'd never said it, he told her, "Well, with or without your help, we *are* gonna get him."

"But I gave you the drawing I made of him. How can you imply otherwise?"

Homer's hands were fisted, but he remained silent. "Yes, you did and your drawing is all over the United States. What I'm wondering is whether you drew someone that looked nothing like him and gave him a chance to get further up north."

She looked shocked but said nothing. Neither did Maggie, who could have backed her up.

"Unless he got a boat to Cuba while your guys were chasing their tails looking for him here," Homer quipped.

"Stay out of this. If we want anything from you, we'll let you know." He smiled at Carolyn when he said, "Now, let's get back to you. If that drawing really is of the suspect, it was too good for you to have had just a quick glance at him. So we're wondering whether you met in your condo building or did you know each other back in the Carolinas?"

"How dare you insinuate that I know that man?"

"Well, don't you?" The smile was still pasted on his face.

"No! I never saw him before the night of the murder." She sighed deeply. "Actually, that's not true." She looked up at Homer, who was so angry she was afraid he'd hit the detective. His eyebrows shot up at her last remark. She shook her head slowly, a sign not missed by the officers.

"What do you mean? And, was Homer in on it with you?" This was the first time she'd heard Sargeant Short's deeper voice and it startled her.

"What are you talking about?" She was trying to remain calm, but was finding it more difficult. "Homer wasn't even in the building when I saw him."

"Don't let him get to you. He's just blowing smoke, because to tell the truth, they don't have a clue where to find the guy or who he is."

"I told you to stay out of this, Wiley."

"Well, then, have your clown here leave me out of it. Where'd the chief find him, anyway?" His sneer for Short got a rise out of the man, but the lieutenant put up a hand toward him. "As for Carolyn, she was asked and answered. End of story." He wanted so much to punch his old friend, and even more so the arrogant sargeant, but his fisted hands remained on the table.

"Okay, let's start over." Ignoring Homer, he asked, "Where did you meet the suspect, and let's tell the truth this time. You said it wasn't true that you only saw him once."

"But, I am telling the truth, Lieutenant. I thought I first saw him when we collided as I was stepping off the elevator, but I just remembered seeing him another time when I was on – on the penthouse floor."

The detectives looked at each other, and then Butler asked, "You were visiting the victim?"

"No, I had a piece of mail for his neighbor that was put into my box by mistake. You can check with the neighbor, Chris Gilliam, and he'll confirm it."

"We'll do that. Now, what's his name?"

"I just told you. Chris . . ."

"Not him," he snapped. "What's the killer's name?"

"How would I know his name? And, I didn't say he was the killer. I just said he was running down the hall that day and collided with me. He didn't stop running long enough to introduce himself."

"No need to be sarcastic, ma'am. I'm only trying to get some answers, here."

"Yes, you asked and I answered – multiple times. Why don't you believe me?"

"Because there's more to the story than you're tellin'."

"Dammit, if you're not going to arrest her, I'd like you to leave now."

"No, please, I want to answer his questions."

"Don't you see what he's trying to do? He's going to keep badgering you, until he somehow trips you up, and then he'll haul you to Stock Island and throw away the key."

Shaking her head, she said, "He can't trip me up when there's only one answer to his questions, the truth." He frowned, but said no more.

"Now, do you have any more questions for me that I *haven't* answer at least twice?" she asked.

"Yeah, as a matter of fact, I do. Where did you meet the suspect?"

"Dammit, Butler!"

Again she shook her head at Homer, as Maggie tugged at his arm. They both feared he was going to be taken back to jail if he kept interfering. Taking a very deep breath and exhaling slowing, she looked the detective in the eye and repeated, "Once again, Lieutenant, I never met the suspect. I saw him briefly about a month ago, walking toward Mr. Strummond's door, as I was handing the mail to Chris. I left right away and can't even say whether he went inside the victim's apartment. The next time I saw him, he ran into me as I was exiting the elevator the night of the murder. He never spoke and neither did I, so I don't know his name and I've never heard the sound of his voice. That's the whole story and if you ask me one more time, I'm calling my lawyer."

Running his hand through his hair, the lieutenant took a deep breath, also, and then finished his coffee. He held his cup out to Maggie, who got up and refilled it, grudgingly. After she sat back down, he mumbled his thanks, looked at her and said, "Okay, let's get to your part in this fiasco. Were you in on it from the beginning or did Ms. Cramer involve you after the murder?"

Maggie laughed, and said nothing, as Homer's fingernails dug into his hands. She put her hand on one of his and patted it. The lieutenant repeated the question, and still Maggie said nothing.

"Look, either you answer my questions here, or we can take you back to the jail and ask them later."

"Lieutenant, I don't know even why you're asking me that question and I don't understand what you mean by it."

"It's a simple question, ma'am. Were you in on this murder during the planning stages or did she get you involved after it happened?"

"Wow, that's one of those when did you stop beating your wife questions? No, I was not in on the murder before or after it happened. Now, are you satisfied?" Homer chuckled when she glanced over at him.

"No, I'm not satisfied. If you weren't in on it, why did you go to Ms. Cramer's condo right after it happened?"

"Well, now, I think even you could figure that one out." She smiled sweetly at him, and once again, his face turned beet red, and he tugged at his tight collar. He had to get some of this weight off. Damn clothes were all too tight, lately, he thought as he chomped down on another glazed donut.

"I'd like to hear your answer now, Ms. Metronia, or I'm leaving this house with you in handcuffs."

Homer jumped up and started around the table. Carolyn grabbed his hand and stopped him. "Please, for Maggie's sake."

The man sat down, but murder remained in his eyes. He'd never cared much for Blake Butler when they were younger, and he'd sure like to knock his lights out now. The nerve of the guy, badgering two helpless women like this. Why in hell wasn't he out looking for the real killer? He said so aloud.

Butler cleared his throat, ignoring Homer's words and venomous look. "Ms. Metronia, why don't you tell us why you went to see Ms. Cramer."

"To find out what she knew about the murder in her building, of course. Since it sounded like the same guy who killed poor Jackie and that other man, I thought if I talked with her, maybe she'd remember having heard or seen something that would help us find the guy."

"Us? You're admitting you and Homer were conducting your own investigation after being told to butt out of it?"

"Homer was doing nothing, Lieutenant. He didn't even know I'd left the house when I went to Carolyn's condo. In fact, he'd ordered me not to leave the house or get involved with the investigation. He threatened to take me somewhere way up the mainland if I left. And, for that matter, I wasn't conducting an investigation. I was just curious as to whether Carolyn had heard or seen anything."

"That's bullshit and you know it." He looked at his notes. "You said, and I quote: 'I thought if I talked with her, maybe she would have heard or seen something that would help us find the guy.'"

"Okay, maybe those were the words I used, but I didn't mean them literally. I meant if she remembered something, we could go to you with it. That's all."

"Yeah, that's why the two of you conducted your little private stakeout. Right?"

"Well, yes. We thought if she saw him again, we could let you know."

"But, you did see him again, and instead of letting us know, you started to follow the guy. Right?"

"Well – Homer called you, didn't he?"

"Yeah, but he wasn't in on the stakeout now, was he?"

"Not really. I mean, no, of course, he wasn't."

"So, what were you going to do if you caught up with the guy, since you obviously had no intention of involving the police?"

"But, we *were* going to call you, Lieutenant," Carolyn interjected.

"I'm not talking to you, now, Ms. Cramer," Butler said, pleasantly. "I want to hear what Ms. Metronia has to say about all this. Answer the question, please, ma'am."

Maggie smiled at him and said just as pleasantly, "I already answered the question."

"Well, let's pretend I'm hard of hearing and need you to repeat your answer."

"My answer is that if we'd caught up with him, we would have called the police and told them where he was."

Short glared at her. "You're a liar."

"Now, wait just one cotton-pickin' minute! You can't talk to Maggie that way. No one on this island shows her that kind of disrespect!"

"Shut your trap. I'm a cop and I can talk to her however I like."

Putting his hand on his sargeant's arm, his superior office smiled at Maggie. "I agree with Homer, Sarge. You're being a bit harsh on Ms. Maggie here. My apologies for Sgt. Short, Ma'am. Sometimes he gets a little hot under the collar and says the first thing that comes into his head."

Maggie roared with laughter, until her eyes filled with tears.

"What's so damned funny?" Short's nostrils flared and his face was blood red.

Ignoring him, she turned back to Butler. "I love your good cop, bad cop routine, It's almost as good as they do it on 'Law and Order: SVU'," she told him, laughing again.

The lieutenant flushed. "I don't know what you're talking about. I was just apologizing for my sargeant's bad behavior. He misspoke and that's all there was to it. We're playing no games here, I assure you." He glared, as Homer laughed aloud.

"Mag's got your number all right. Now, are you through with this so-called interview? If you are, I'd sure like you to leave."

"We're not through, Homer, and we're not leaving."

"Well, you're on private property and without a warrant, I'm within my rights to ask you to leave."

"Just one more question, and then we'll go." He turned from Maggie and his eyes pierced Carolyn's. Lowering his voice to almost a whisper, he asked, "Did you kill Mr. Strummond?"

Her hand went to her throat and her face blanched as stark white as Homer's counters she'd been staring at. She rose to her feet and swayed. Homer hurried to her, and put his arm around her shoulders to steady her. Maggie handed him a glass of water, and he held it to her lips. She sipped, and then thanked him with a nod.

Ignoring that tableau, the detective went on, louder this time. "It's a simple question, Ms. Cramer."

"No, Lieutenant, I did not kill Mr. Strummond or any other human being in my life. I could never do such a thing. I've never owned a gun. And, you can search my apartment right now and you won't find any knives missing. I'll give you written permission to search. You'll find all of them in the butcher block, where they belong." The color was returning to her face, as she spit the words at the detective.

"Did you help the suspect plan the murder of Mr. Strummond, then?"

"Oh for God's sake, Blake!"

"I'm asking her, not you. Did you help him plan the murder?"

"No, I did not."

"All right, she's answered all your questions – several times. Now, I'm asking you to leave my home or I'm calling my attorney right now." Homer stood and moved toward the officers, with his cell out, punching in numbers. They backed away from the table.

"Okay, we're leaving, but I need to tell the three of you again, don't leave the Keys." Homer slammed the door behind them, as soon as they walked outside.

"Damn cops!" He went back to the kitchen to make sure the ladies were all right.

TEN

"Look, guys, we're getting nowhere on this case. It's been three days since those two saw the person who ran into Carolyn Cramer the day of the murder. We questioned her every which way but she stuck to her story." The lieutenant cleared his throat. "I'm sure she's telling the truth. We blocked off the Keys as soon as Homer called us, and yet, there's not been a nibble. I know he was being factitious when he said the guy's probably on a boat to Cuba, but I'm thinking he might not be far off the mark."

"Hell, if that's true, he's right that we're just blowing smoke out there searching for the guy."

"Maybe not." He paced the room, his hands linked behind his back, as his sargeant and the other detectives stared at him.

"What're you thinkin'?"

He smiled at Short, as he stroked his lower jaw. "Well, I'm thinking we could make him a CI and maybe even let him go undercover for us . . ."

"Surely, you're not talking about Wiley." The entire squad wore incredulous faces just like Sgt. Short's.

"Don't look so shocked. The guy was a Marine, he has good instincts and I think he'd do a damn good job for us long-term as an informant."

The room filled with agitated murmurs. Homer Wiley was a smart guy, but few of them thought they could trust him. Chief Lenny Doan was observing them from behind his glass petitioned office. It wasn't often the entire room was buzzing like that. Curious, he started to open his door, but thought better of it. Butler will fill him in if there's any news or a change in the game plan.

"Right now, we could send him into Cuba from Cancun, pay him well and have him shack up in Havana for however long it takes to scout the whole island. We could send Shirley to . . ."

"Oh no! "The officer jumped out of her chair, sending it crashing to the floor. No one bothered to pick it up, but some of the men were grinning. She pushed her hand, palm out toward him. "No," she repeated. "I'd rather quit the force as team up with Homer Wiley. Why would you even suggest that? You know his reputation with the women."

Shirley Savage was a leggy 40-something redhead who'd been working vice for ten years. She was invaluable as an undercover officer. She could change her looks faster than most men put their second leg into their pants in the morning. Whether the job called for a sexy blonde or the darkest shade of brunette, there was no hesitation. She didn't care if she had to wear an Afro or have dred locks that smelled to high heaven. She'd be in the salon chair within five minutes. No wigs for that woman. If it called for her to be a wrinkled homeless senior, she'd be under the wing of their best makeup artist for hours, if that's what it took to age her thirty years. She loved the job and thought she was the luckiest woman on the planet. Most days. Today wasn't one of them.

"Take it easy, Shirl. We're not saying you have to share a bed with the guy. Just make it look like you are. I've known Homer since we were barely out of our teens, and I'd trust him with my sister. Wouldn't like it, but I'd trust him not to hurt her."

"She-it, Lieutenant, you know I've never refused a job in my career."
He grinned at her. "Yeah, I know."

"Can I at least have a day to think about it?"

"Sure. Why don't you take the rest of the day off, go home or somewhere else relaxing? Have a few drinks with a friend. Or just go to the beach by yourself." His smile then turned into the fiercest look she'd seen out of him. "Take all the time you need, but I want an answer by tomorrow morning, Savage. If this guy has slipped into Cuba, we have to know now. We can't afford for his murder spree – if he is the killer – to expand to other countries. We'd never get him back if that happened."

"Okay, boss. I'll give it some serious thought." She got out of her chair, and headed for the door."

"Oh, Savage? Might not hurt to have them make you into a really dark brunette while you're at it."

"But I didn't . . ."

"I get it." He threw up his hands and bowed his head. "You want to think about it first. But we'll want the two of you on a plane to Cancun tomorrow afternoon, so the sooner you start making the change, the better. Don't get a haircut, though. Homer likes long hair on his women."

She glared at him and went out the door muttering one curse after another, as the rest of the room erupted in laughter. "Okay, settle down. We have work to do. I don't want to let up on any of our surveillance here just because we're going to expand it to Cuba. And, Davidson?"

"Yeah?"

"You take the rest of the day off, too. I want you on the same plane as Savage and Wiley."

The young narcotics officer grinned from ear to ear. "You serious? Me go to Cuba?"

"That's what I said. If they encounter the guy, and he turns on them, I don't want Shirley the only person holding a weapon."

"Why not swear in Wiley? I'm sure having been such a good Marine, he knows his way around weapons?"

"I have no doubt of that, but I don't know if I wanna take it that far. I'll talk to the Chief now and get his take on it. Regardless, I still want you to go as backup. You don't need to pretend you don't know the two of them. All three of you will arrive on the island together and be inseparable after you arrive."

"Okay, if that's what you want."

"Find a place where all of you can share the same room – or suite, if there is such an accommodation over there. Use your own names, since he's known on the island, but the two of them will be a couple. You're all good divers, so you can do a lot of diving, dancing, whatever it takes to blend in. Not saying not to drink, but keep it in moderation. I need you both alert at all times. Got that?"

"Sure, no problem," the young man told his boss. He was the best looking man on the force, and had just celebrated his 26th birthday. He'd joined the Key West Police Department straight out of Key West High School, and never looked back. Being a cop came naturally to him and he'd quickly moved up to Narcotics, being undercover longer than he'd worn a uniform. "But, why can't I be the boyfriend? You know I'm better lookin' than Wiley." His grin was splitting his face, and the rest of the squad laughed.

"Yeah, and about as vain as he is, too," Butler told him, joining in on the laughter. "Go on, get outta here and start packing. I'll give you a call when it's firmed up."

"You got it. See you later."

"Okay, guys, get back out there. Maybe the perp's still hanging around the island, after all. We can't let up and just assume Homer's right that he's on a boat to Cuba or already there."

After they left, Short turned to him. "Are you sure about this, boss? I'm not too keen on using Wiley as a CI, much less having him go undercover."

"What alternative do we have? Neither the SO nor us has a clue where this guy could be hiding."

"Yeah, but still – Wiley?"

"I don't think we have a choice. Homer Wiley is our best bet right now. He speaks good Spanish, and I think he'd be a natural. No one would think twice about his turning up on the island. Everyone likes him and he's certainly had his share of Cuban girlfriends. Come on, let's go talk with the Chief to see if he knows any rich ol' geezer on the island who'll front the money for us to send that trio to Cuba."

His sergeant laughed. "I wondered where all that money was coming from. It sure wouldn't come from the department, as much as the chief is always begging the city commission for funds for this and that project or equipment."

ELEVEN

"You're out of your ever-loving' mind, Lenny! I wouldn't mind bein' paid to inform you guys, but go undercover with those clowns?"

"Come on, you want this guy as much as we do. You know he's a possible threat to your friends."

Homer scratched his silver crew cut and said, "Sure, I'm worried to death about Mag and Carolyn."

"Well, we've thought a lot about what you said, even though I know it was said in jest."

"I said a lot of things."

"True, but I'm talking about the guy being in Cuba by this time. And, we think you could very well be right."

"Huh?"

"Think about it. As soon as you called us, the entire Keys and the mainland were placed on high alert, yet no one turned up a trace of him."

Homer sneered. "Yeah, I've noticed."

"Well, he could have a boat or, at least, had his eye on one in case he needed to get off the island in a hurry. I think it's worth it to have the three of you fly over and blend in with the locals, diving, fishing, drinking – whatever – for as long as it takes to cover the whole island, the surrounding coves and out-islands."

"I'd do that better by myself. Everyone's used to seeing me over there."

"I thought you'd never been there before."

He grinned. "That's just what I told Maggie."

"Regardless, you can't do this alone. We'll cover all your expenses for months if that's what it takes. You'll have unlimited available funds. The bills will come directly to this department." Homer's eyebrows rose at that caveat. "No one will know who's paying the bills, since they'll go to a post office box we've set up, the funds provided by an interested benefactor, who wishes to remain anonymous."

"But what about Mag and Carolyn?"

"What about them?"

"You know Maggie. If I'm not there to keep tabs on them every day, she and Carolyn with her, will go out on their own again to find this guy. God only knows what kind of trouble they could get into."

"True, if that's possible."

"And, he might figure out they're alone and come after them here."

"I've already got that covered, Wiley. Two of your 'cousins' are visiting from Maine. They're on extended leave from another cousin's company during the slow season, so they can stay in Key West for several months."

"What!"

The chief ignored him. "You just had a death in Colorado. Since you were named executor of your deceased uncle's estate, you have to fly out and stay there until everything's settled."

"Colorado? I thought you said Cuba."

"Don't get ahead of me, Homer. Your cousins didn't know him, because they're from your mother's side of the family, so no one would wonder why they didn't go with you, if anyone even notices you aren't home and two strangers are living in your house."

He ran a hand through his silver crew cut, as he stared at two seagulls that suddenly appeared on the windowsill. When they flew off again, he blinked and asked, "Who's gonna take on that job?"

"Two of our best sharpshooters – George Snow and Ken Lambert. I don't think you've met Snow, but you've known Lambert for years.

Snow came to us from Philly and he's got a sharp eye, just like Kenny. The women will be safe with them."

"Shit," Homer said, almost to himself. He was out of excuses. And, he did want to get that sonofabitch who'd frightened Carolyn so badly, before he hurts her, and possibly Maggie, too. He'd do anything to keep them safe. He stared at a spot on his sandal for a long time.

"Well?"

He raised his head and stared at the chief of police. His shoulders heaved with a sigh. "You've got me over a barrel and you know it. When do you want us to leave?"

"You'll stay at the Airport Hilton tonight. You're on a plane to Cancun, leaving MIA at 4 tomorrow."

"You sure don't waste any time, do you? Well, I guess I have some packing to do." He grinned. "Like I said, Mag still thinks I've never been to Cuba, but I sneak off every now and then to visit old friends on the island. Been going over since I was in my late teens."

"I figured that with all your Cuban girlfriends. Why the ruse where Maggie's concerned?"

"Just trying again to keep her out of trouble. I don't always stay in the nicest places down there. And Mag – well, it's bad enough with her, as it is. You wouldn't believe what she – never mind," he said, with a big laugh. "When do you want me to go to Miami?"

"Joey's rented a vehicle and he'll pick you up at noon."

"Noon today?"

"That's right. I told you we'd booked you into the Miami Hilton tonight. The three of you will have plenty of time to get comfortable with each other."

"Right."

"Come on, man. You'll enjoy playing Shirley's boyfriend. She's a sassy lady and I know you'll get along just fine." He grinned at Homer who'd never seen the charming detective, but his expression was sullen.

"I'll be waiting for them to show. When are my 'cousins' coming in?"

"They're already at the house waiting to surprise you. Maggie and Carolyn have been briefed on what's going down, and they're fine with it. I spoke with them, myself, before you got here."

*

"Hey, cuz, long time no see," Sgt. Ken Lambert said, grabbing him in a bear hug, as he whispered into his ear, "Play along. We haven't finished sweeping the place, yet."

"Yeah, Hom, it's been a really long time. What were we, ten and sixteen?"

Homer glared at the younger man and motioned for the women to follow him outside. The men watched from the deck doorway after they finished looking for *bugs* inside the house. "Are you sure the two of you are okay with this?"

Carolyn spoke for them. "Yes. You just go over there and find this guy. We'll be fine. 'Jake' and 'Garrett' have been telling us stories of your escapades as young boys, and we've been laughing for hours," she said to reassure him they could handle and, in fact, were going to enjoy the company of Snow and Lambert, who were turning out to be great actors and making up stories as they went along.

"Yes, we'll be fine. We all want this over with. If this is a way to fish him out, then you're just the fisherman to do it," Maggie told him with her big toothless grin, getting smiles from the two men standing in the doorway, more than ready to take over guard duty for Homer.

Stepping outside, Lambert interrupted. "Maggie's packed everything she knows you like to take with you to another island, so why don't you come back inside, have a drink and relax till your ride gets here, buddy."

"I'll relax after we get that guy, Lambert. Hell, this might just be a waste of everyone's time. He might be holed up with a girlfriend right here under our noses, for all we know."

"And, if he is, they'll find him," Snow told him with too much of a brilliant smile. He disliked the guy on the spot. Too pretty to be a cop. Nothing overtly tough-looking about him. "No one in the Keys is going to let up on their surveillance."

Homer ignored him, and went straight to the deck bar to grab a frosty Sam Adams. He drank most of it in one gulp, as the others watched him, looking at each other with concern. Maggie went over to him and put her hand on his arm. In a barely perceptible voice, she said, "We'll be just fine. They've already warned us they won't let us out of their sight, so what could go wrong?" He said nothing, just glared at all of them.

"One of them's sleeping in your room and the other there on the sleeper in the Florida room, so no one's going to get into your house. Please, don't worry," Carolyn assured him.

He turned and smiled at her. "I know. Doesn't mean I gotta like it." He looked at Maggie with concern. He messed around with glasses on the counter to muffle his voice. "Just you make sure you have each other's backs, okay?"

"I won't let Maggie out of my sight, and since the guys won't let either of us out of theirs, nothing will go wrong."

"Somehow, I wish you hadn't said that. I know from experience Mag exists on Murphy's Law."

Lambert grinned and walked over to the deck bar. He took out a Sam Adams. After taking a swig and turning up the already loud music, he looked at his old friend. Their relationship had for years been a mixed bag of both pleasant and contentious.

Finally, he spoke. "We won't let you down, pal. You've known me too long to know I'd ever do less than my best for you. And Georgie-boy here might look like a softie, but he's a crack shot and has an eye like an eagle. He also can hear a pin drop to the pavement outside, when he's inside a building."

"I know. Lenny assured me of that. It's not that I don't want to do it; I'm just anxious about leaving them when the perp might not have left the island, after all."

"We're going to be their shadows. They'll get so tired of your *long-lost cousins* they'll be praying for you to get back."

Homer laughed then, and Cpl. Snow walked over, bent down and pulled out a Corona from the outdoor fridge tucked inside the front of the bar. "Sarge is right. We're gonna stick like 'Elmer's Glue' to these ladies. We'll make it fun for them, as much as we can, and before you know it, it'll all be over and you all can get back to your lives."

Homer turned, hesitated for a moment, but then shook the man's hand. "Thanks, Snow."

"Just in case, maybe you'd better use 'Jake' and 'Garrett' when you call to check on the ladies. We haven't uncovered any bugs, but one could always be planted when we're gone." He looked at Homer, but the man still seemed unconvinced.

"We'll close up the house nice and tight and make sure the alarm's on before we go out to dinner or wherever, but he could always get onto the patio and access the phone line that way."

"That's what I'm afraid of." He continued to stare at a flock of snow-white egrets on the far side of the next finger canal.

"We'll keep checking each time we return to the house, so try not to worry. Just play the game and we'll all be fine. Since you'll be using your cell to call, anyway, he won't know you're not in Denver, if he even gets wind of your 'uncle' passing."

Homer didn't smile, but he knew what Snow was saying was true, that Maggie and Carolyn would be even safer there with the two officers than they'd been with him. He tried to relax and look forward to going back to Cuba. He still pretended to Maggie he'd never been there before. He'd try to see it through her eyes and maybe the time would go faster, he told her.

He'd have good company, he thought with hesitation, not knowing Shirley Savage, but figuring if Lenny was sending her with him, she'd be such a competent undercover officer, she'd become a great girlfriend while they were there. It had been awhile since he'd had a young woman to keep steady company with, something he was beginning to like about having Carolyn Cramer living in the house.

Maggie watched him carefully, and she breathed a big sigh of relief as she saw his expression becoming one of acceptance. She'd seen Officer Savage and knew he wouldn't mind one bit being in her company on that beautiful island. She was about his height, with gorgeous slender shapely legs, more than easy on the eye from the waist up, too, and thick long hair he'd enjoy running his fingers through – if she let him near her, that is. She could see how feisty she could be with her co-workers. Homer might balk at the assignment, but he'll enjoy the challenge of Shirley Savage, after it begins.

TWELVE

"**W**ell, ladies, it looks like the chief was right in thinking Homer was onto something when he mentioned Cuba. They've found no more *vics* since the one in your building, Carolyn, so it's a pretty sure bet he isn't here on the island, anymore."

They were sitting in the shade under the large banyan in Homer's side yard off the deck, which wrapped around from the back of the house. The women were finishing their iced tea and the men, more of Homer's Sam Adams.

"It does look that way, doesn't it," Carolyn told *Jake,* with a smile.

They'd been cautioned not to let their guard down on calling them by their fictitious names so the women usually didn't call them by name, because despite their doing complete sweeps of Homer's house and boat, they still might miss a bug if the guy who planted it were clever and inventive enough. Even when that far away from the house and deck, they never used their real names, despite feeling safer talking about the case there.

"I'm convinced Homer was right, too. Sure, all you guys laughed when he mentioned it, but as one of you said, he has great instincts, and they're usually right on the money."

"Despite being one of those who laughed about it," *'Garrett'* told Maggie, "I'm becoming convinced he was right, too. I hate to admit it, but sometimes Homer Wiley can be a big asset to the department."

Maggie laughed. "Better not let him hear you say that. I love that boy, but he's vain enough as it is."

Her three companions laughed with her. "Sometimes, I think that's all for show, Mag. I think it's a cover to keep away those who might care about him. He's afraid he'll be hurt if he lets anyone, except you, get too close."

"Hmm, never thought of it that way before," she told the other woman. She'd been looking at Snow in a strange way for several minutes, so he said something about it.

"What is it, Maggie? Why are you looking at me like that?"

"Oh, I'm sorry. It just dawned on me that you remind me of my godson Timmy."

"He must be a good lookin' guy then, right?" He laughed and took another swallow of his Corona.

She teared up and said, "Yes, he was, but he was shot and killed in a drive-by in New Orleans several years ago."

He went to her and held her for a few minutes, as he whispered how sorry he was. "I can tell you really loved him."

"He was the son I was never able to have. You not only look a lot like him, but you have a sweet way about you like he did." She coughed to keep from crying. "He always treated me like I was his real mom, especially after she died."

"I can see why he'd do that. You have a mom-personality," he said with a smile.

'Garrett,' wanting to change the mood that was settling over them, said, "Regardless of his personality quirks, I'm glad the boss made Wily a CI and tapped him for the gig over there with Shirl and Joey, after the lieutenant suggested it. I have to give them credit. It was a real long shot, as far as I was concerned." He had become a fan of Homer Wiley's again when he stepped up to the plate to help nab this guy.

"I couldn't have said it better. Now, let's forget work and take these nice ladies out to dinner. We can take the boat up to Ziggie and Mad Dogs, if you like."

"Haven't been there since Shirl's big birthday blast, so sure, why not."

Maggie looked puzzled. "What and where is Ziggie and Mad Dogs?"

"You've not been there? It's great," Carolyn told her. "We used to go at least once a week when I lived over here. It's a fabulous gulf-side restaurant and bar on Islamorada."

The men looked at her. "I'm surprised you've been there," Snow said.

Laughing, she replied, "I'm not always a stick in the mud."

He grinned and winked at her. "Okay, let's lock the place up tight and get that motor started!"

~ ~ ~

Homer and Joey Davidson climbed back into the boat. "Gee, fellas, I thought you'd gone to sleep down there and the sharks had taken advantage of it."

Davidson grinned. "Would we do that to such a gorgeous companion?"

Homer laughed at the young narc's attempt at flirting. He was getting more overt about it, as the month wore on. He frowned, thinking of how long they'd been in Cuba, without a sign of the mysterious perp who wasn't in the system. No one even knew the guy's name, since the identical fingerprints they found at the last two crime scenes matched no one known to the Monroe S.O., Key West P.D. or the FBI. Nada. Absolutely nothing came up on any of their databases.

"Hey, Wiley, why the long face all of a sudden?"

"Just sick of everyone comin' up empty, I suppose. It'll be a month tomorrow, and here we sit, twiddling our collective thumbs and having a grand old time on the KWPD's benefactor's dime. We don't know any more than we did before we left."

He tossed his flippers onto the deck, as he struggled out of the wetsuit. Shirley watched him in silence. She couldn't figure out whether she liked the guy or not. He could be arrogant and vain as hell, but sometimes he was really sweet, too.

"Don't want to make it worse, buddy, but sometimes I've sat around in the same old grungy rags I've worn for three or four months before I get a nibble," the young man told him. "Heck, once I didn't get to change clothes for seven months. By the time I hit pay dirt, the rags were literally falling off me in pieces."

"I don't know how either of you do it. I'm sure not cut out for this."

Shirley smiled at him. "Oh, I don't know about that. I'm pretty proud of how you've played the game and kept your cool, despite your obvious disappointment in the process."

"Glad you think so, but I feel like a teapot ready to boil over any minute now."

"Understandable." Davidson was getting ready to turn the boat back toward Havana so they could eat dinner."

"Really, how do you do it, day after day, night after night with zero results?"

Joey Davidson looked back at him, before turning the key. "You just occupy your mind with diversions. Sure, ultimately you're always thinking of the goal and what's gonna happen when you reach it, but you'd go mad if you thought about it 24/7."

"I thought that was what you were supposed to do."

"On the surface, yeah. Underneath, in a saner part of your mind, you're thinking about where you want to eat, if you aren't supposed to be homeless and reduced to picking through garbage cans, that is."

"That's it? Just thinking about restaurants? That keeps you sane?"

"No, that's not all you're doing." Shirley was beginning to feel sorry for the guy, despite balking at spending time with him when the assignment came up.

"I don't know what you mean."

"You're thinking about the people you care the most about. You're doing things like we did today. Fun, mundane – easy things to keep our minds active and alert for the real job at hand."

"Yeah, and I'll guarantee you that if and when one of us does spy that sonofabitch, we'll all go into crisis mode and our reactions will be right on the penny," Davidson added. "Even you will surprise yourself."

"Doubt that." Homer wasn't looking at either of them, but out to sea, as the motor purred, scattering dolphin who'd been ahead of them most of the trip. A couple of them back-flipped to either side of the boat and kept its speed.

The cops looked at each other with concern for the first time since they got to Havana, as he continued to talk. "I'm not saying I'll freak out. I keep pretty calm in any crisis. It's a Marine thing."

"Of course, and we're not worried about you freaking out," the other man assured him.

"That aside, I don't know how much good I'm going to be to either of you."

"Relax, Homer," Shirley said, with a hand on his shoulder. "You're going to be fine. We're not worried about it."

"Glad *you're* not."

"Hey, for a rookie undercover agent you're not half-bad."

"A double-entendre if ever I heard one," he told her, laughing. They joined in his laughter, and since they were nearing the dock, Davidson killed the motor. The tide took them the rest of the way, and when they bumped the pilings, Homer jumped out. Between Shirley and him, the lines were secured before the other man finished gathering his diving equipment.

~ ~ ~

Stateside, the two women and their male companions were climbing from Homer's boat onto the dock at Ziggie and Maddogs at mile 83 in Islamorada. The bar was lively as they walked through it.

"Looks like there's no seat left in here, ladies. Any objections to eating outside by the water?"

"Heck no. I prefer it.

"Carolyn?"

"Sure, what're the Keys for if you can't have most of your meals outside by the water, with these balmy breezes kissing your face."

"Okay, that's settled. There's a table for four right there on the far side, closest to the water."

"Why don't you grab it, *Jake*? Carolyn and I need to freshen up a bit." Maggie flashed him her best toothless grin.

Jake' looked at *'Garrett,'* but the other man shrugged. "Sure, why not?"

"Okay, but hurry back, 'cause we want to order. I'm starved," *'Jake'* told them.

"We won't be long." Carolyn bit her lip as she turned around and followed Maggie. She hoped she wasn't up to something else.

"Okay, here's the deal."

"No, absolutely not! No more sleuthing."

"It'll be just a teeny bit. Aren't you sick of spinning our wheels?"

"We all are, but on the other hand, aren't you enjoying our little adventure with the guys on the police department's dollar?"

"That's a given. I can't deny they're great company, and they treat me just as nice as they do you, even though I'm way past young and pretty."

"Oh Maggie. Stop selling yourself short. You've still got a figure twenty year olds envy, with toned arms and legs and that beautiful long hair. Your face is still heart-shaped, with barely perceptible wrinkles. You're very pretty . . ."

"Don't forget to add, 'for your age.'"

"Of course, that's true, but how many other 70 year olds who've never had plastic surgery can say that?"

"And, don't forget to add, 'except for when you open your mouth and smile.'" To emphasize her point, she did just that and Carolyn giggled.

"You're one of a kind. You know that?"

"Yeah, don't think God had any more molds like this one." She laughed with her friend. "Seriously, though, getting back to the little diversion I've got in mind."

"Please, let's just go back to the table, have a nice dinner and forget about the case for awhile."

Maggie shrugged. "Okay, we can do that. For now," she added, as she stepped out of the ladies room, with Carolyn tagging behind, looking relieved, the men thought as they spied them.

"Wonder what that's all about," *'Garrett'* said, as he stuffed a piece of flatbread laden with Cajun Crawfish Dip into his mouth.

Both of them stood and pulled out the chairs for the women, who told them thanks at the same time. They sat back down and Maggie asked, "What's good for dinner?"

"We're starting out with the crawfish dip, but if either of you want another appetizer, please feel free." He shot his younger partner a look, and almost imperceptibly, shook his head.

"No, this looks real good," the oldest member of the group told him.

"It is, Mag."

"What were you two thinking for the entrée?"

Wiping the dip off his face, *Jake'* said, " *'Garrett'* here is going for the New York strip, but I was thinking of having Alaskan King crab, myself. You ladies get anything your little hearts desire." He winked at Carolyn, whose face suffused a little.

"Yes, that sounds good to me, as well. Mag?"

"Grilled salmon for me, guys."

They nibbled on the flatbread and dip and talked about everything that came into their minds, except why they were together. Their eyes kept surveying the packed patio, though, and the older of the two men took on dining room surveillance, as Carolyn and Maggie kept visual contact with the bar. The younger man watched the door. Soon their entrees came, and they busied themselves with napkins and utensils.

The women and the handsome young narc sipped Sauvignon Blanc, while the older officer enjoyed Cabernet with his steak. They nonchalantly conversed and surveyed their surroundings at all times. Still, by the time the night was beginning to show its bright stars and full moon, and they had long since finished with their entrees and Key Lime pie, nothing. Not a sign of the Keys killer, if that's whom the man was who rushed past Carolyn the day of the last murder. Their counterparts in Havana were coming up empty, as well.

THIRTEEN

"Maybe we're climbing up the wrong tree, Homer. Maybe he's nowhere near Havana."

"Cuba's a large island. He could be just about anywhere on it, or on the out-islands surrounding it."

"I didn't expect it to be this big," Shirley interjected. "After living on Key West, this is huge. I doubt we've covered half of it."

Homer laughed. "Half? Try a quarter. "

"I can see why the chief told us to stay months, if that's what it takes. Geez Louise, we're never gonna get to everywhere."

Homer clapped him on the back. "We'll get there, man. Just try to relax and enjoy it, as you both told me to do. You could have spent thousands to stay here just one week, you know. Besides, aren't we supposed to be on vacation? We don't want to look as though we're in a hurry to get to anywhere, do we?"

"Yeah, I guess for an undercover cop, I'm not as patient as I try to pretend, sometimes." His partners laughed at him, and Homer pointed to a small building where he said they could get some great *cajita*.

They walked to the door and Shirley whispered, "Homer, this isn't a restaurant. People live here."

Homer laughed and asked whether they preferred beef or pork.

"Beef for me."

"I don't eat much meat, but when I do, it's usually pork," Shirley told him.

Homer beckoned them to the doorway and walked inside. They waited while the older Cuban woman he called Mama went into her kitchen, as he played with her young grandchildren. The children, ranging from three to five seemed to know him well and were climbing all over him as though he were a tree. He laughed easily with them, shocking his companions who'd never seen this side of him.

When their weathered *abuela* returned to the main room, she carried three boxes and sets of utensils for them. Homer gave her three dollars worth of *pesos* and a kiss on her wrinkled cheek. She kissed him back, and patted his cheek with a big smile. After he handed Shirley and Joey the boxes, he reached into his backpack, pulled out a large envelope and gave it to the woman. "*Gracias, mi amigo*," she said, and gave him a hug.

"*Da nada*, Mama." They turned to leave when he turned back to the woman, as though he'd forgotten something. He had. He reached back into the backpack and gave her a photo of the man they were looking for. She looked puzzled and then shook her head no after Homer said something else to her in Spanish. Then she shook her head yes, and he gave her another kiss, before turning back to Shirley and Joey.

"Is she a relative, Homer?" She thought she might have been his mother the way he acted toward her.

"No, Carmelita's just a woman I've known since I was in my late teens and started coming over here. She's a sweetheart and has always treated me like a son, especially right after we met and I didn't have two dimes to scrape together. She took care of me. Put me up and fed me, until I found a little part time job. And" he said, as he reached into his food box, "she makes the best *cajitas* on the island." He ate a piece of beef and steered them to a large tree in the courtyard, where they sat on a worn piece of wooden bench that wrapped around its huge trunk.

As they enjoyed the rice, fried plantains and vegetables that came with their meat, although they were laughing and joking with each other, their eyes were constantly searching their surroundings for the man they hoped to find. "Now that was a great meal! I can easily believe she's the best cook in Cuba. By the way, what was in the envelope, if you don't mind my asking?"

He looked at her, as though contemplating just how much to tell her. "Just a few *pesos* to tide her over till my next visit. It takes a lot to feed all those kids. She makes a little on her *cajitas*, but I always get more *pesos* than I need when I come over, so there's enough for her. Her husband left the family decades ago for a floozy from Brazil. Her only son, the children's father, died almost three years ago and his American wife went back to Chicago not long after that."

"But the children?"

"Their mama didn't want them, and to tell the truth, Joey, she'd have had a hard time getting them all out of Cuba, so it's just as well she didn't try. Mama loves them as fiercely as they do her and takes good care of them."

"How long ago did she leave them?" Shirley wasn't married, but she knew if she ever had children, they'd want for nothing and would have her love and devotion until the day she died.

"I don't know – guess it's been two and a half years now, since Pedro was just six months old when she left. He was just beginning to try to crawl."

"God, it must have been so hard for all of them. I can't begin to imagine how they must have felt when she walked out the door and never came back."

"It wasn't easy, but they have loads of extended family who immediately took to mothering them, along with their grandmamma, who wouldn't let them out of her sight for a minute."

"But, surely no one can take the place of one's own mother so quickly."

"Oh, they missed her like crazy," he told her. "And the baby cried all the time for a while. He was still nursing when she left, so they had to get a wet nurse for him. But as you can see, they've all survived and are happy and thriving under their *abuela's* care. They're lucky to have her."

"That's just plain sad. Makes you wonder why some women have babies in the first place. I can see wanting to go home after her husband died, but to leave her children behind? Just can't wrap my mind around that." He shook his head, before taking the last bite of his meat.

"They're better off here, Joey. Who knows what kind of life they'd have had with Sally, even if she'd wanted them and found a way to get them off the island." He stood up after gathering their stainless utensils. "I'll take these back to Mama and then we'll be on our way."

They stopped and had *Mojitos* at a small hotel bar after they'd walked for a while without seeing anyone resembling their guy. "I want to find that guy and get outa here. I'm really getting antsy, fellas."

Homer laughed, and told her, "Hey, I've got a good cure for that, if you'd just say the word."

"In your dreams, bagpiper."

Joey laughed at the two of them. "Tell the bartender we'd like another round. I'm still dry."

After their third *Mojito*, they decided to go back to the *casa particular* and call it a day. The private home they stayed in was licensed for lodging, and the food was much better, Homer told them before they landed on the island, than at any of the hotels around. He'd called the one he usually stayed in, and they sent someone with an old van to meet their plane. Occasionally he stayed in a room in a more run-down part of Havana, but he didn't think it would be suitable for Shirley Savage.

"Maybe tomorrow we'll try Chinatown."

"Do you really think he'd go there?"

"I have no idea. It's about the only place in Havana we haven't spent any time in since we landed."

She shrugged. Joey asked him what their options were if they came up empty in Chinatown.

"Well, if we have no luck there, we'll check out of the house and go over to Camaguey for a while. If he's familiar with Cuba, he might find that a better hiding place."

"How so?"

"Because if he did come over and wanted to avoid the capital, there are some areas in the eastern side of the island that tourists don't like to frequent, or they just don't know about them. It might be safer for him there, especially if he happens to have any contacts in the hills. The capital city, also called Camaguey, is the most popular spot in the province, but he'd be more likely to hang out further inland away from the city."

Joey didn't say anything, so Homer continued to talk. He knew the two of them were getting tired of being dragged all over the big island without having any luck, and he didn't blame them. Neither of them had ever been to Cuba. Couldn't speak the language, so that in itself had to be frustrating. The size, alone, was overwhelming compared to Key West, especially when they had to cover all of it.

"We know he isn't in Cienfuegos or Santi Spiritus, or any of the others in the center of Cuba. And, you're right," he told him. "We've covered everywhere on the western side he could have come. Well, except for Chinatown. So, if he's not there, but is on the island, it has to be somewhere in the east."

Joey brightened all of a sudden. "Now that I think about it, seems like Camaguey was the place where my grandparents had a beach home till the early '50s."

"Does your family still own it?"

"No, I think when the Batista regime fell to Castro, even though they complained about Batista's dictatorship, they saw the writing on the wall and got the heck out of Dodge."

"Did they just leave the home to Castro and never look back?" Shirley asked.

"No, they had the deed with them, since they'd owned it for around twenty years, and just quit-claimed it to a good Cuban friend for helping them get off the island in one piece."

"Why? Were Castro's rebels after them?"

"No, but they were over here when he took over, and they regretted not having left before, since he and his thugs were making it pretty rough on everyone."

"So, you never got to come over here to visit them in the beach house."

"No, 'fraid not. I wasn't even a whisper in my mama's thoughts, yet. I wasn't born until nearly twenty years after he took over."

"That's a shame they had to give up the house." Homer was thinking how nice it would be if he had a home of his own to come to there.

"I don't know. I doubt they'd ever have come back even after things settled down some. And, then with the embargo, well, I don't think they'd have gone to all the trouble of flying to Cancun and coming in the back door the way you and Maggie do."

"So, they died without ever seeing their winter home again?"

"That's right," he told her.

"That's just sad."

"Yeah, it was, but they adjusted to it and rarely mentioned the island again."

They reached their rooms and Joey suggested they hang out in his until they got sleepy. "I need to win back some of my bucks from last night's poker game, anyway. So what do you say?"

"Not me. I'm sleepy from all those drinks, and couldn't stay awake to play cards if you paid me to do it, never mind winning. Goodnight."

They told her goodnight, and Homer followed Joey into his room. "She's looking pretty peaked, isn't she?"

"She's okay. She's done undercover for more years than any of us on the force. She just gets tired of night after night without any results quicker than the rest of us."

"Why'd she choose to go that route then? Surely she'd like other parts of law enforcement better."

"Can't answer that. She's been offered plum spots since I've been there, which hasn't been that many years. I thought she'd take the sex crimes position that came up when Margo left the force. She would have been in charge had she taken it."

"When was that?"

"About two years ago, I think. Margo'd been there for twenty, at least. Shirl started out working sex crimes with her, in fact. She was good at it, too, from what I hear."

"Why do you think she turned it down?"

"By then, she'd worked undercover on just about every case we had and I guess it just appealed to her more."

"She sure doesn't act like she enjoys it much."

"Don't let her fool you. She'd rather be out here pretending she wasn't a cop, than to be working anything else on the force."

"If you say so. Well, let's get a few hands in before we turn in. By the way, what time are we hitting the streets again?"

"Better set your alarm for three. I know Shirl'll be pounding on our doors by then, if not before. By now, you know it only takes three or four hours of sleep and she's raring to go again."

"Yeah, I've noticed. Oh well, whose deal is it?"

FOURTEEN

"I wish I hadn't let you talk me into this."

"Don't be a spoilsport. It'll be fun. And, the guys will still be sleeping when we get back. They won't even know we've been gone."

"What did you put in those beers, anyway?"

Maggie laughed and told her she'd laced them with a couple Seconals each.

"What! Where did you get Seconal?"

"I had to have a little outpatient surgery a few years back. It was over so quickly I didn't even tell Homer about it. I took 6 of them home with me when I called the cab. The doc thought I'd have trouble sleeping. I don't like to take anything that makes me fuzzy, so I still had the whole bottle in my cabinet. I grabbed it before I left the house with Homer, after we got out of the hoosegal."

"Hoosegal?"

"Yeah, you know, the slammer, the jail."

"I think I've laughed more since I teamed up with you, than I had in forty years of living on this planet," Carolyn said, with a giggle.

"Well, if it makes you smile, that's fine with me. You hadn't smiled much before then, you know. Maybe Homer has something to do with that." Her grin was impish, and Carolyn threw up her hand in protest.

"I'm happy the way I am, my friend. I don't need anyone trying to set me up with any man. I don't want to be miserable again, even though Homer's a nice guy."

"You could do worse, you know."

"Maggie, let's get on with it, okay. I'm not interested."

"Okay. Let's park over there on Caroline where the tourists park. No one would think to look for us there. We could have a drink at one of the tables by the open windows next to the dock in Turtle Kraal. That way we'd see everyone who goes by."

After they'd been served and talked for a while, Carolyn said, "Don't look now, but there's Lt. Butler over there talking to the chief."

"Where? I don't see him."

"There," She pointed to the Rawbar. "See, they're talking to that woman who just came out of the place."

"Oh, yeah, now I see them. Well, are you almost through with your drink? I guess we'd better mingle with the crowd and make our way back to the car."

"Yes, I've had enough. We don't need them harassing us. Let's hurry before they come this way."

Maggie thought for a moment and then said, "We'll sneak through the public parking lot, once we leave the walkway."

Safely through the parking lot, from Caroline, they turned up Eaton, and found a spot to park near Island Books. From there, they walked to The Bull, and ducked inside. They sat at the far side of the bar, where they could see both Duval and Caroline. That wall of the bar was one big open window and it was easy to spot anyone on the street and sidewalks.

"What'll it be, ladies?"

"I'd like a grasshopper," Maggie told him.

Carolyn smiled , and ordered a Scotch on the rocks. When the bartender walked away, she asked, "Doesn't it make you sick to drink so many different things in one night?" It was the fourth drink they'd had, and each time, Maggie's was different from the last.

"Naw, I can drink 'bout anything you'd hand me. Liquor's liquor, ain't it. Don't make me no never mind." Her voice was beginning to slur, as was her usually good command of the English language.

Carolyn laughed and then turned somber. "Do you really think he's still on the island?"

"I don't have the slightest idea, but looking for him beats sittin' around the house, doin' nothing."

"Have to agree with you there, but it just seems like we'd have seen him by now, if he'd stayed around that day."

"Homer's probably right about the guy hopping a boat to Cuba, but we can't just give up our search here."

"Maggie, may I remind you that we've been told to butt out and let the cops do the searching? They told us their surveillance is still active."

"I know, but we've got eyes the same as they have and we found him the first time, didn't we?"

"Yes, but he got away, too, remember. The chief was adamant we stay out of it and let them do their job."

"You got that right, little lady."

The two women nearly choked on their drinks as a beefy hand clamped down on a shoulder of each of them. "What are we going to do with you two? And, where the heck are Snow and Lambert?"

"Oh, hi, Sargeant Short. How are you tonight?"

"Stuff it, Ms. Metronia. Where are the officers?"

"They – well, they were sleeping when we left. We weren't sleepy and were bored with just sitting around watching TV. We just wanted to get out of the house for awhile."

"Were you not instructed to go nowhere without them?" He looked at Carolyn, his face a snarl.

"Well, yes, we were, but ..."

"No buts about it. Orders are orders. Maybe I should just throw the two of you in jail for the night, and then we'll see if you're able to follow our instructions better if and when you get out." He pulled the handcuffs from his belt, and put them on both Maggie and Carolyn, as others in the bar continued sipping their drinks as though nothing else were going on.

"Oh no, please, we'll go back home now. We're really sorry if we did something wrong. We didn't think anyone would mind if we came into town for a drink," a now-stone-cold-sober Maggie said.

"Nice try."

"Please, I'll see that we stay put. After all, I'm the one who drove us here."

"You bet your life you'll stay put. Come on, let's go to your car. Charlie," he told the other detective, "we'll walk to their car, and then you'll drive it behind mine. I'll take them with me. The keys, Ms. Cramer."

He held out his hand and Carolyn, looking even more frightened than Maggie, who could scarcely take a breath for fear of being locked up again, dropped her keys into it.

When they got back to Sugarloaf, and were standing by the sargeant's car, Short asked, "Do the guys always sleep so soundly that the two of you can just walk out without them hearing you?"

"Oh yes, sir. Sometimes we're making all kinds of racket and they're just dead to the world," she told him, innocence dripping like syrup from her lips. Carolyn remained silent.

"Is that true?" he asked, looking back her.

"Uh, yes, sometimes they drink a lot of beer when we're out on the boat and they do sleep very well."

"Yeah, right."

Charlie Perdue laughed, and looked at Short. "Do ya think maybe the guys had a little help from the ladies?"

His partner glanced at him and opened the back door of the car. He didn't bother taking either of the women out, though. "I've not a doubt in the world."

Maggie and Carolyn looked at each other. Carolyn was shaking her head. Why had she been foolish enough to be talked into leaving the house after Maggie drugged the two detectives?

"Do you remember the penalty for drugging someone?" Short was enjoying this. It had been a quiet night until they spied the two sitting at the bar. "Isn't it something like fifteen to life?"

With a twinkle in his eye, the other man said, "Yeah, I'm pretty sure that's what the judge gave that guy last week and it is on the books."

The women gasped audibly. Carolyn had never had anything like this happen to her before. She could barely take a breath.

"I think you're right, my friend. But, maybe he'll go easy on them, seeing as how they're otherwise nice ladies. Maybe he'll settle on thirty or so each."

"I don't know. It wasn't just anybody they drugged, after all. It was police officers."

"Yeah, I hadn't thought of that aspect of it. I'm afraid he's really gonna go hard on them for that."

Still not a word from the back seat. Neither woman realized the detectives had no intention of arresting them for anything, but were simply trying to put the fear of jail into them, so they'd stay put. Their main concern was that the perpetrator had not gone to Cuba and might recognize Carolyn Cramer. They didn't want any harm to come to either woman.

"Let's hope not. I know they realize now they were wrong to do it, but who knows. He might just decide to throw away the key this time to make an example of them. Maybe they really are looking at life instead of a few decades."

Purdue could barely keep from laughing, as he heard the deep rapid breathing from in back of him, despite the humming cicadas in Homer's trees. They'd scared those two so badly he didn't think they'd even go to the ladies room without asking permission from now on.

"Well, let's go see if we can wake those clowns up."

FIFTEEN

They let the women out of the car, but kept the cuffs on. When they went inside, there wasn't a sound to be heard. Playing along with the plan, they called out to 'Jake' and 'Garrett,' in case they'd been drugged so heavily that the place had been bugged while they were under and the women were away.

"Wha – what's going on, Short?" 'Garrett' walked out of his room in a hurry, shocked to see the two detectives standing there, and more so, that the women were cuffed.

"Well, we found your lady friends down at The Bull, and wondered why they weren't escorted."

'Garrett's' eyes widened, but he didn't say anything. He realized immediately what he'd done.

"I don't know what you're talking about, Officer." At least 'Jake' was awake and alert enough not to act like he knew Short. He glared at his partner. "Do you, 'Garrett'?"

"No, I don't understand what's happening."

"Let's go outside and sit in the night air. Maybe that'll wake you clowns up, and you'll remember there's a killer on the loose in Key West."

When they were outside, where there wouldn't be any bugs to record them, he yelled, "Hey, Charlie, make our friends some coffee, will ya?"

"Okay, coffee comin'up. I guess you don't want to let the ladies out of cuffs long enough to make it, huh?"

"Cuffs? Why're they in cuffs? For heaven's sake, take them off."

"No, we need to keep 'em on. And, they're in cuffs, because we found them alone in Old Town. We'll probably be taking them to lockup as soon as we get the story from you guys."

"Aw, come on," 'Jake' said, "they didn't mean any harm, for God's sake. Take them off 'em."

"Sorry, no can do. We have to find out why you weren't with them, before we take them to lockup."

"Yeah, they're innocent in all this. Don't do that. It's our fault they were out on their own," 'Garrett' told him.

The women sat on the wicker glider, both of them still so scared their legs were shaking. The two men were sick about it, and couldn't understand why the sargeant was being such a prick.

"Okay, forget about the ladies. I want to hear why the two of you were sleeping so soundly you didn't hear them go out the door, much less drive away. Didn't you hear the car start?"

"No, we'd have stopped them had we known they were going. I think we must have gotten some bad beer or something. I never sleep like that. Hell, if I sleep three hours without waking up, I'm doing good."

"What about you? Did you get some bad beer, too?"

"I must have. Like 'Jake,' I never slept like that. Ever."

Short sat back and steepled his hands, as his arms rested on the arms of the deck chair. "Well, let me tell you what I think happened. I don't know where they got 'em, but I think your sweet innocent ladies there ground up some sleeping pills, dropped the powder into your last beers, and shook it up real good."

"Aw, come on, they couldn't have done that. Besides . . ."

The cop interrupted 'Garrett.' "And because you'd had a few too many to begin with, I think when you drank the last ones you both just went out like someone turned off a light switch. Then, when they saw you were both dead to the world, the two sweet little ladies somehow dragged your sorry asses into your room to let you sleep it off."

"But . . ."

"And then, while you were both in la-la land, they grabbed the keys, ran for the car and sped off for the island, so they could resume their little spy game again. How does that sound to you?"

"Yeah, sound about right, guys?" Neither of them cared for Charlie Purdue and couldn't understand why the lieutenant promoted him to detective. His scores weren't so great that he deserved the job. There were plenty of other cops out there who would have made better detectives.

"Stuff it, Purdue," 'Jake' said, not caring what the sargeant thought.

"Okay, watch it, man. We're not here to be harassed by 'civilians.' We need to get to the bottom of what happened tonight to make the two of you sleep like the dead, while the two people you're supposed to be guarding take off to play undercover cops."

"Keep him off my back," he told Sgt Short. He rubbed his neck. His head was splitting in two. He didn't know what Maggie slipped into their drinks, but it must have been a doozy. "We told you we don't know what was wrong with the beers, but something was. I highly doubt either Mag or Carolyn know a drug dealer, much less how to go about getting drugs to put into our drinks."

"Besides," 'Garrett' added, "they've not been out of our sight – well, until tonight, that is. When could they have bought drugs when we've been on them like fleas on the dogs Homer doesn't have?"

"All right, all right, just can it. You've no more idea what happened than we do. Ladies, you're off the hook this time. But I swear, we see you in Key West or anywhere else without these two guys with you one more time, you're gonna be taken to jail, no questions asked. No arguments and no more favors. Got that?"

"Yes, sir. I promise we'll do what you say."

"How 'bout you?"

"Absolutely, sir. Carolyn's right. We'll do as you say and stick right with 'Jake' and 'Garrett' from now on, until this is over. I promise."

"You sure as hell *better* promise and stick to it, or there'll be no more nice conversations – nothing. You'll be taken right back to that cell and the judge will throw the book at you this time. I'm keeping a record of what happened here tonight, so just keep that in mind." He glared at them.

"And, as for you two. You'd better keep a closer eye on them or you'll be fired and brought up on charges of neglect – or whatever else I can come up with." He smiled and winked at both of them, since his back was to Maggie and Carolyn.

Finally catching on, 'Garrett' said, "Sure, Sarge, we're really sorry about tonight. You have our promise it won't happen again. We'll stick like glue to both of them."

"You'd better. Let's get these cuffs off 'em; we're outta here."

The women were rubbing their wrists after Purdue took off the cuffs. They were not saying a word until after those two detectives were gone.

After they were gone, 'Garrett' looked at Maggie. "She-it, woman! What in thunder did you do to us?"

"I'm sorry."

"But, how did you get drugs? You hadn't been anywhere without us."

"I had an old bottle of Seconal with six capsules in it from the hospital after I had surgery."

"Are there any left?"

"Yes, two," she said, with a whisper.

"What! You put two Seconal in each of our beers?" 'Jake' shouted it at her.

"I knew they wouldn't hurt you."

"Like hell you knew! What if one of us had been allergic? Did that even occur to you? Chri . . ."

"Come on, man, she said she was sorry. Neither of us was harmed, so let's just drop it. They've been through enough tonight. Is there any apple pie left from dinner?"

"Yes, half of it's still in the fridge. You want some?" Carolyn glanced at Maggie when she said that, because she was still trembling.

"Yeah, thanks. Fix us each some hot apple pie and some decaf, please." He rubbed his eyes to try to focus better, but his vision was still blurred. "Throw a little vanilla bean on top of it, while you're at it. We all just need to calm down and let the med wear off. What's done is done, and it isn't going to happen again, right?"

"Right," two voices said at the same time.

"Okay, then, let's just forget it and start over. Okay?"

'Jake' smiled and said, "All right, but I'll tell you both, if you ever even think about slipping anything into my drink again, I won't wait for Short and Purdue. I'll haul you to jail, myself."

"We understand. It won't happen again."

"It better not." Then, turning from her to glare at Maggie, he said, "I want those last two pills. Now."

Her eyes widened, and she hurried from the deck to her bathroom. She brought the bottle back to him. He took the two small capsules, opened them and stomped the contents under his shoe. Then, he took a paper towel, wet it and picked up the finely crushed medication. He carried it into the house and threw it down the commode in the half-bathroom off the main hallway, making sure there was none left on the paper towel. Seeing none, he smiled to himself, rinsed it and threw it into the small waste can before going into the kitchen to join the others for pie and coffee.

SIXTEEN

"Jake,' thanks for not making a bigger deal out of my – you know."

He smiled and patted her hand. "I couldn't stay mad at you, Mama."

"That's sweet. Where does your mom live, by the way? I've never heard you mention her."

He turned a little pale and she asked, "What? What did I say?"

"It wasn't anything you said, Mag. It's just that – my mom, she died a long time ago."

He seemed not to want to discuss it any further, so she patted his hand and said, simply, "I'm sorry, dear."

Not wanting to bring everybody down, he brightened and asked, "What do you say we spend today on the water?"

"Sounds good to me. What about you ladies? Up for some sun and fun?"

Carolyn looked at Maggie, who had a dubious look on her face. "What's wrong?"

"I don't know. Why don't the three of you go? I'm not really in the mood this morning."

"Hey, that doesn't sound like our Maggie. What's got you down, luv? Not what I said about my mom, I hope."

"No, it's not that," she told him. "I'm still shaky from that run-in with Short and Purdue, I suppose. That guy gives me the creeps."

"Purdue?" She shook her head yes. "Well, he's not my favorite cup of tea, either, but I'm not going to let him ruin my day."

"Me, neither. You shouldn't let what happened with them spoil one more minute of your life. I don't think Homer would like knowing you're moping around and we didn't do anything to help."

She smiled at 'Garrett.' "Okay, I'll go, though my heart isn't in it. Give me a minute to change."

"That's the spirit. I'll pack some lunch and we'll be waiting on the dock."

"Okay." She smiled at her friend, and went to her room.

"Thanks for suggesting this," Carolyn told 'Garrett' as she threw a picnic lunch together. "She really needs it. I've never seen her this down before. I'd give anything if I'd not gone along with her little spy outing, yesterday."

"Don't kick yourself for it. We all know how headstrong she is. She'da gotten around it, somehow, even if she had to walk into town."

"I suppose you're right. Let's just forget it, here she comes."

Maggie's smile was bright as she walked toward them. No need to drag the rest of them down. They all returned the smile. The two undercover cops had gotten used to that toothless smile and thought nothing of it, now. They'd both fallen in love with her over the past few weeks and accepted the whole package.

As they glided along with the motor humming, the dolphins joined them on one side of the boat, making Maggie laugh at their acrobatics. This made her companions relax. Despite the smile, they knew her heart wasn't in the ride, but the dolphin always cheered her up, and it was no different today.

They were going south into the Florida Straits, with no particular destination in mind. The sea was unusually calm, even in the straits, where one could always count on rougher waters. The sun's warmth and the soft breezes kissing their faces made them relax even more.

Carolyn, who was terrified of the creatures in the sea, even had her hand trailing in the warm water, to 'Jake's' surprise when he glanced over at her, but he didn't allude to it. He was glad she and Maggie were having a nice time. Yesterday seemed to be forgotten.

Around 1:30, 'Garrett' said he was getting hungry, so Carolyn grabbed the picnic basket and set up their lunch on the small table in the cabin. 'Jake' opened their beers, after he dropped anchor in a small cove.

"This is nice. I'm glad you all talked me into coming."

"We needed it today, Mag," Carolyn told her. "I'm glad Homer gave us the use of the boat."

"Did you do a lot of boating when you lived on Sugarloaf?"

"No, not a lot. I'd never cared much for it before."

"Any particular reason," 'Jake' asked, after he swallowed the rest of his turkey sandwich and washed it down with a big swig of Sam Adams.

"Not really. To tell the truth, I think it was just spending time with the man I was married to that turned me off. Not getting into specifics, but we just weren't very close."

He shrugged and let that one pass. "You seem to like it just fine, now."

She gave 'Garrett' a big smile. "Yes, I have to admit I've enjoyed it. Maybe it's because it's a diversion from the real reason we're all together."

Her friend smiled at her. "It's certainly that. Homer never could get me out on it. That'll change now that I know how relaxing it is."

"Good for you both. There's nothing like being out on this open sea with no land in sight to put things into perspective."

"You have that right, pal. I never had a boat before, but after this gig's over, that's the first thing I'm going to look for. My life's gonna change big time." 'Jake's co-worker looked at him with a puzzled expression. "No more going to work and not going home until things calm down. I'm going to start enjoying these beautiful Florida Keys after all this is finished."

"You sound like you're not just talking about a boat. Are you thinking of quitting the force?"

"Nah, nothing like that. But, I've been thinking of hangin' up the undercover gig. Just buy a little boat and work regular shifts so I can enjoy it, instead of not seeing my place for days, and sometimes months on end."

"Wow, that's a surprise! Can't say I blame you, though. You're young and have plenty of time to do this old man's work." His partner gave him a fatherly smile. The younger man turned away to hide a sudden welling up in his eyes.

"You okay?" Carolyn didn't miss the tears.

"Huh? Oh sure. I'm fine. Something just blew into my eye and I needed to turn from the wind. Throw me another can of beer, please, will you?"

~ ~ ~

"Hey, look there – three o'clock – the guy on that dark blue skiff."

"I think you're right, Homer. Turn a little in that direction. Not enough that he suspects anything, but just enough to get us closer to be sure it's him."

Homer negotiated their small cabin cruiser closer. They'd had it jazzed up by an old friend of his to run like a cigar boat, if necessary. He stayed back and to port side of the other boater. He even waved to him, as Joey and Shirley pretended to be kissing and not paying any attention to either of them. He waved back to Homer and got a little further ahead of them.

"I don't think he suspects anything. I gotta tell you, though; I got a real good look when he turned and waved back to me. I'm certain he's our guy. What do you want me to do now?"

"Just stay calm and act casual, as you're doing. We have all the time in the world. We want him to think we're out here enjoying the water just like he is. Let him get ahead a good distance."

Shirley asked, "Anyone want anything to drink? I'm going to get a water."

They both told her no, so she went down to the galley. While there, even though Joey hadn't mentioned doing it, she got on her cell to Butler. She gave him their coordinates, and was told that he and the chief were also on the water, and Snow and Lambert were just about a hundred yards south of them, with the ladies in the boat.

"We'll alert them and rendezvous with them toward you. Keep doing what you're doing. Wait for my call before you let him know you're cops. We have to let him get into our waters before we make a move toward him. We don't want the Cubans comin' after us and him getting away again."

When she returned to the bridge, she saw Homer was staying behind and to the west of the alleged perp, but steady on his course. "Think he still doesn't suspect anything?"

"No," he yelled over the loud motor, "he's not sped up or changed course, at all. I think it'll be a real surprise when he finds out who we are."

She told the other officer, "I called Butler while I was in the galley. He and the chief were already on the water, and said Snow and Lambert are ahead of him with the two women. Homer's not gonna like that, so better not say anything to him just yet. Butler said to wait for his signal before revealing our hand."

Davidson glanced over at her, but didn't say anything. Was he upset that she called? She said nothing, but handed him a water, even though they'd both said they didn't want anything. "Thanks, Shirl. Guess I could stand a drink, after all."

"Figured you could."

His grin reassured her. "Thanks for alerting the lieutenant. It's good to know we have four others backing us up, in case things get rough out here. Who knows what kind of arsenal the guy might have."

She relaxed, after he thanked her. "You're welcome, Joe." She walked to the bow, and offered another bottle to their captain. "Homer?"

He glanced around and saw what she had. "Thanks. Set it right there, hon. I'll take it in a few minutes."

"Might make him believe you're relaxed if you're sipping on something, you know." She smiled and he grinned back at her.

"Guess you're right, at that." He took the bottle and opened it, taking a long gulp before putting it back on the console. "Thanks, it tastes good."

"You're welcome."

SEVENTEEN

"What the . . ." I see my boat heading toward us. My God, Mag and Carolyn are on it. Who put them put into this position?" He yelled, "Joey, will you call to warn them, so they can take the women out of range?"

"No can do. Shirl called Lt. Butler. He told her he was with the chief a few yards behind the guys. They know Maggie and Carolyn are in the boat and I'm sure they'll take no risks. You just have to trust all of us to do our jobs."

"Dammit! Doesn't look like I have a choice, does it." They watched, as Carolyn got lower in the boat. They remembered the perp had seen her getting off the elevator. In the distance, the police cruiser was gaining and moving to the east, without its blue lights on. They'd have him surrounded when they made their move. Homer wished Maggie would get down, too, but then that might look too suspicious, if suddenly both of them did it. He hoped she was careful.

Joey's cell rang, and he put it on speaker. "Yeah, Chief?"

"Davidson, you and Savage get ready to pull your weapons. Homer, don't change your speed, but get just a little more to the east. We don't want him to have room to reverse his direction."

"Got it, Lenny."

All of a sudden, they heard him on the bullhorn. "You there – turn off your engine. This is the Key West Police Department. We have you surrounded."

The man looked panicky and at first gunned his motor. "I repeat; turn off your engine!"

They heard it turn off and the man's hands went into the air, as all three boats moved next to his. Then, he spied Homer's boat with the two officers and Maggie and Carolyn. He yelled, "It's him! He made me help him!"

A shot rang out and the man ducked. Shirley said, "What the hell? Who fired at him?"

They heard the chief yell. "Stop firing! He's surrendering! Stop firing now!" Another shot rang out and they saw that it came from George Snow's weapon. "Snow, drop your weapon. Now!"

He fired again, getting the unknown boater in the shoulder and he fell to the deck. Then, to everyone's surprise, Maggie reached out and grabbed for Snow's revolver. "Stay out of this, Mag." He slammed his boot into her leg and she buckled. She didn't fall, but made another grab for the gun. He dodged to her left and as if in slow motion, they all watched in horror, as she went overboard.

Homer yelled, "I've got her!" He dove off the boat into the water where he last saw her, before anyone could blink. In a couple of minutes, he came up for air, took a large gulp and then dove back into the water, which still was relatively calm on the surface. He repeated this a couple more times and then, to everyone's relief, he came up with the woman. She looked like she wasn't breathing. Shirley, who'd been a medic in the Navy, reached down. Together, they got her into the police boat. She'd jumped into it, ready to do what it took to keep Maggie alive until they reached the hospital.

Joey had climbed into the other boat while this was going on, and cuffed the unknown boater, as the chief and Butler jumped into Homer's boat to assist Ken Lambert, who was struggling to get the gun from Officer Snow. He managed to choke Lambert with his free arm, causing him to black out for a moment. Loose again, he got to his feet, with his gun trained on the chief and lieutenant. He looked to his right, saw Carolyn, frozen with fright, and grabbed her, his gun to her head.

With a calmness he didn't feel, Lenny Doan said, "You don't want to do this, George. Give me the gun and let us help you. I don't know what you've gotten yourself into, but nothing's worth this."

"You're way too late, Chief. No one can help me now."

Carolyn was so frightened her legs were visibly shaking. She looked like she might faint at any moment. Lambert was just coming to, but still too dizzy to stand. While the chief distracted the younger officer, Butler inched further to his right. He was in position to grab his arm when Snow noticed him. He turned the gun from Carolyn to him.

This was enough of a distraction that the chief was able to grab Carolyn and pull her out of range. Snow didn't want to hurt her, or anyone else for that matter. There'd been enough killing. He was so tired. He just needed to stay calm, give himself a chance to think.

"You know I don't want to hurt you. Come on, drop the weapon and let's talk about this."

"And, I don't want to hurt you, either, Lieutenant, but I will if you come any closer. You, too, Chief."

"For the love of God, son, will you put down your weapon and talk to us. We're all your friends. We want to help you."

"I appreciate your friendship and your position, sir, but I'm way beyond help. Just get back on your boat, so I don't have to hurt anyone. Please," he pleaded, tears shimmering in his eyes.

"All right, you win. We'll go, but first you have to let Butler get Ms. Cramer safely over to the cruiser."

Snow didn't say anything, but motioned with his weapon for the lieutenant to do as the chief asked. Butler wasted no time. By then, their boat had moved close enough that both Savage and Davidson were in position to jump aboard. Snow yelled at them to stay back, so they didn't move, but kept their weapons drawn.

After Carolyn was safely on the police cruiser, the lieutenant told her to get on the floor and stay there, until he told her it was safe to stand again. He kept his weapon trained on the young officer as the chief tried to talk him down. The other two did the same, as Homer tended to Maggie.

"Why'd you have to be so damned brave?" He was relieved when he saw her eyes flutter open at that moment and her breathing increase a bit. "Oh God, Mag."

"I – I'm sorry."

"But, why'd you do it?"

"I didn't want him to shoot the man, anymore – or hurt any of you. Was the closest to him, had to take – chance."

"Your chance might have gotten you killed, woman. Don't you ever do anything like that again!"

"I won't."

"You'd better not!"

"God, I was so scared when he dodged me and I went overboard."

"I'm sure you were."

"You know I'm not that great a swimmer," she added, with a small smile. He was pleased that her voice was stronger, and there was some color back in her cheeks.

"Yeah, I know." He grinned at her then. "What *you* didn't know was that Jaws might have made a meal of you before you drowned, had I not found you when I did. Two of them were circling from a distance, right before I grabbed you."

She gasped and turned white, again. She was remembering their close call with the alligator in the mangroves across from Alabama Jack's. She'd thought she'd bought the farm then, and couldn't believe how close she'd been to it again.

"Chances are they'd not have attacked, but I'm glad I was close enough to the boat that Shirley could grab my hand. It would have been hard to deal with two of them, had I had to, and still keep you afloat."

"I'm so tired – just have to – sleep awhile."

He panicked. "No, you have to stay awake. Try to get some sips of water down. You have to wait till we get back home before you can sleep."

"Okay." She took a couple small sips of water. "Did he hurt anyone else?"

"No, he let Blake Butler take Carolyn to the police cruiser, and the chief's trying to talk him into giving up his weapon now."

"Why'd he do it? Do you think – could he be involved with the murder of those men?"

"We're not sure of anything at this point, hon. It looks like he was, though. The guy we were looking for accused him. And, since he shot at him multiple times, I'm afraid there's some truth to what the guy was saying."

"He was so nice to us, Homer. I hate to think he's one of the bad guys. That he'd do something as horrendous as what was done to poor Jackie and the other two men."

"We all do, but looks like he is – for some crazy reason we don't yet know."

EIGHTEEN

"Come on, Chief, get back on your boat and let me go. Please. I promise no one else is going to die. You have my word that it's over. Just let me go and I won't come near the island again. I promise. I'll head straight for Brazil."

"George, you're a cop. You know I can't do that. Just talk to me. Make me understand what your part is in these awful homicides.

Snow said nothing. The chief ran one hand through his hair, while the other still held his drawn weapon. "I just want you to be okay."

"I don't deserve your kindness. Just get back on the boat and I'll get far away from you and the others. I won't come back to the states, I promise." He swiped at a tear and repeated, "There'll be no more killing. You have my word on that."

Doan took a deep breath and exhaled slowly. "Okay, I'll do that, if you'll do something in return."

The young detective looked wary, but agreed. He hoped he could do what the chief was going to ask, because he just wanted it to be over. He was exhausted from the strain of pretending to be a good cop, knowing the opposite was true.

"I just want one thing – for you to tell me why. That's all. Just try to explain why you, the best undercover officer we've ever had on the force, would do something like that. Or was it the other man who did it, and you just paid him off?"

George Snow slumped slightly, but kept his hand on his revolver. "No, chief, I paid him to help me, but it was both of us who killed them."

"But, why? Why would you do something so heinous?" He kept his eyes averted from Butler whom he'd watched, in his peripheral vision, quietly climb back aboard the boat way to the stern. Lambert was still struggling to sit up, so he couldn't depend upon him to help subdue their disturbed friend. The lieutenant was afraid Snow would see him, as well, and he'd be forced to shoot him before he could disarm him. That was Lenny Doan's worst-case scenario, too, his greatest fear at the moment. That he or Butler would be forced to shoot him. Beads of sweat pierced the skin of his forehead, and ran down the sides of his face.

"I had nothing against Jackie or the trucker, Chief. I'm real sorry for including them in my plan to get him."

"Who? Strummond?"

"Yeah. It was that bastard I was after. Been after him for the past twenty years. I figured if we took down someone known and cared about by everyone in the Keys, it would distract everyone's attention until I got to him. The trucker just happened to be in the wrong place at the wrong time. He saw what we'd done to Jackie. We had no choice, but to do him, too."

"But why Strummond? What did he do that was so terrible he deserved to die like that?"

The young man sneered. "What'd he do? For starters, he stole my damned childhood. I was only six years old when I had to watch from my mother's closet as the bastard tied her up with wire. He raped her until she passed out, and then slapped her face until he got her to come to. After he raped her again, he slit her throat with a machete. The last thing she did before she took her last breath was – was turn her eyes toward the closet where she'd hidden me. I knew she was trying to tell me to stay there and not to make a sound. And" he sobbed, "I know – I know she was trying to – to tell me goodbye."

"My God!"

"Oh, but he didn't stop there. He turned up the stereo real loud and started cutting off every part of her he could get to, as he danced to the music."

"Jesus!" The Chief made the sign of the cross with his hand that wasn't holding the weapon.

"All the while, I was holding my hand over my mouth and vomiting into it. He couldn't hear me over the music. If he'd known I was in there, I'm sure he'd have done the same to me. That would have been worse on my mother, if she was still alive when he was butchering her, but I wasn't thinking about that then. And to tell the truth, I've wished every damn day of my miserable life he'd found me and put me out of it then instead of my having to grow up, reliving that nightmare every day of this miserable existence," he said, sobbing harder.

"Oh God, George," the chief said, with tears threatening to spill from his eyes.

"He slaughtered my mother like she was a pig, Chief. Then, he raped her again after she was dead, laughed like it was the funniest thing in the world, wiped his machete and bloody hands on the bedspread and walked out the sliding glass doors."

Snow was weeping hard now, and all the officers and the women felt deep sorrow for this man they'd all come to care about and to respect as the fine police detective he was. Between sobs, he asked, "Is Maggie okay? I didn't mean to send her overboard. I just wanted her to get away from me so she'd not get hurt."

"She's going to be fine, "the chief told him.

"Thank God," the younger officer said, and then wept harder. Despite holding their weapons on him, every officer involved had tear-filled eyes. They could hear Carolyn's sobs from the police boat.

"So, he was never caught."

"Oh yeah, he was caught all right. Covered in my mother's blood. Someone called the cops and they caught him before he got to the edge of town. We lived in Jacksonville at the time."

"Didn't the state attorney file his case? This doesn't make sense."

"He filed and the judge took it to trial. He was convicted on several counts of sexual assault and first degree murder."

"Don't tell me. He was such a model prisoner, they let him out in ten years."

"No, he was denied parole twice. They allowed me to attend each of his parole hearings. He thought that was comical and laughed heinously at them for allowing it. Then, one night, he managed to escape through a hole he'd been digging patiently with a piece of his bed that had been loose when they threw him into his cell."

"But, I've never heard of or seen an escape bulletin of anyone by the name of Walter Strummond."

"No, you haven't. But, I'll bet you've seen 'em for Victor Marrow."

The chief's face blanched. "Walter Strummond was Victor Marrow? That's impossible. His prints didn't match anyone in the system."

"Did you notice the burn scars on his arms and hands? All self-inflicted."

"Yeah, but we still were able to get some partials, though to tell you the truth, there wasn't much to them, so nothing substantial went through the system."

"I had to laugh when I noticed he'd been burned. Told him, as he was dying, what a piss poor job he did of it. That he should have had the plastic surgeon do a better job, instead of burning his own hands."

He stopped for a moment, wiped the sweat from his brow with the back of his hand that held the gun, and said, "It took me a few years of stalking him to make sure it was Marrow, but I'd have known him anywhere. His long chin hadn't changed that much, and he had this gross hairy wart on his back that was as big as a black cherry. He should have had that removed, too, while he was at it – or just not have indulged himself by stripping off his shirt and soaking up the sun like he loved to do at the Casa Marina beach after he moved to the island."

"How long did you stalk him?"

"Oh lord, it must have been at least ten months this last time. It seemed every time I got to observe him up close and personal, Dispatch called and I'd have to leave him to his self-indulgence. That's when I decided to ask for undercover. I knew I'd be bothered a lot less if I did that. Finally, with more time on my hands, I was able to follow him and find out where he lived."

"Why didn't you come to me when you realized you'd found an escapee? We could have gotten him and he would have paid for what he did to your mother."

"I thought about that for awhile. But then deep down I knew nothing they'd do to him would make him suffer like he made Mom suffer, even if he did go back to prison." He wiped sweat from his forehead with the hand that held the gun. Butler moved and he turned the gun on him, so he sank back down to the deck.

"No, I wanted to watch him writhe in pain. I wanted him to feel what my beautiful young mother felt as he was torturing her. I wanted to keep him alive as long as possible, so he'd scream out like she did, but with the gag stifling his screams, just as his tape did hers. Didn't want anyone else to hear them and come to the bastard's rescue." The tears were running down his cheeks in steady streams now and he swiped at them.

The chief was horrified with what he was hearing, as was everyone else, except Maggie, who'd passed out again on the other boat. He said nothing and the young officer continued his story of horror.

"You know, Mom was only twenty-six years old. She didn't deserve such a horrible death, but he did. I made sure he got it, too, and don't expect any remorse from me, because I don't have an ounce of pity for the bastard. I do regret with all my heart killing Jackie Weener and that trucker. If I had it to do over again, I'd have never killed either of them." His sobbing grew even worse, but he tried to pull himself together to finish saying what he wanted them to know. "Jackie had always been nice to me, even fed me on the sly when he saw me undercover as a homeless guy. He'd not say a word to give me away, but would go into Fausto's, order a good solid meal from the deli and bring it out to me, as though he did it for every homeless person he saw. Shoot, knowing Jackie, maybe he did, but he knew I wasn't homeless. He just wanted me to eat a decent meal. God, I wish we hadn't killed him. He didn't deserve it and I wish I could tell him again how sorry I am, only this time I'd let him go." He swiped at his eyes with the hand not holding his revolver. It didn't help, as the tears were too copious to stop them.

"I'm so terribly sorry for all your mother went through, and for all you've gone through all these years, son. I just wish you didn't have to pay for what that monster did."

"Nothing anyone could do to me would be worse than what I went through in that closet, too scared and too big a coward to help my own mother."

"But you were a little boy! You'd only been on this earth for six years! Nothing you could have done could have helped your mother. For all you know, he would have killed you first and made her watch. At least she was spared that."

The man said nothing, but then, he raised his weapon again. This time, it was aimed at his own head, no one else's. "No, George! No!"

"Goodbye, Chief. Lieutenant. Lambert. Thanks for caring."

Butler lunged, almost reaching the gun, but he was too late. They all watched in horror as their colleague and friend blew the top of his head off and fell into the sea. The chief and lieutenant jumped in and pulled him out, but it was too late to save his life. The chief held him close to him, so overcome that he sobbed like a baby. Everyone else was gulping back his and her own tears, as they watched in silence. As heinous as his crimes were, they didn't negate the fact that he'd been their brother and they cared for him as one.

Savage and Davidson tied the other prisoner's boat to the police cruiser, and Butler started the engine. Lambert, whose dizziness had cleared by then, steered the chief and Snow's body back to Key West, as Butler and Homer followed behind in the police cruiser, no one saying a word. What they'd witnessed was too horrible to discount it with words.

Maggie dozed, despite Homer's best efforts to keep her awake. Her vital signs were getting stronger, though, so he let her sleep. It had been a blessing in disguise, because he didn't think she could have taken it to watch their friend die like that. He hated that Carolyn had witnessed it.

She awakened five kilometers from Key West. "Is everyone okay?"

"Yeah, Mag, it's all over and we're on the way home. Why don't you go back to sleep. I'll wake you when we get there."

"I think I will. I'm just glad it's over and everyone's okay."

NINETEEN

"**H**ow is she?" Lenny Doan asked when they got to the dock, behind the cruiser.

"She's good, Chief." He dug his hands deeper into his pockets, his eyes on the deck. "I can't tell you how sorry I am. Snow seemed like a really good cop and Maggie told me he was good to them while they were all staying at the house."

"Thanks. He was one of our best. Uh – does Mag know he . . ."

"No, thankfully, she'd fallen asleep before then. I'll get her home and tell her when she's fully recovered from her dip in the sea."

"After they've finished checking her in the ER, you probably can take her home. She was quite the hero out there, going up against a man with a gun. As for Mr. Jeffrey Battles over there, he's left holding the bag, and I'm sure the judge won't be lenient with him."

"Even if it was Snow's idea to kill them?"

"Yes, even with that. He's still facing three counts of false imprisonment and first-degree homicide. Too bad he's the only one who'll have to pay, but he doesn't deserve leniency."

"Was he just a bum who jumped at the chance for some easy money?"

"Actually, Homer, it turns out this wasn't his first rodeo. He's a parolee whose real name is Harry Bondare. He did hard time for armed robbery of a bank down in Louisiana, just a mile from his home.

Because of him and his partner, three people, including the armed police guard, died during the robbery. He shot the guard and one of the two women in cold blood. His partner took out the other woman. They'd done nothing to provoke either of them. Witnesses said they laughed and gave each other high fives after they did it. Why he got parole is beyond me."

"Too bad he didn't act alone, and that Snow could still be with us."

"My sentiments, exactly, my friend." The police chief's nose and eyelids were still red from weeping. "Well, they're finished tying up, so I'd better get across the road and help the guys with the paperwork."

"Is – uh – is there anyone who needs to be notified of Snow's death?"

"I wish there had been. Maybe then he could have somehow put that horrifying past behind him. But, no, HR doesn't have a single name, and Shirley, who worked the most with him, told me that he didn't date anyone, either. Told her he wanted to concentrate on the mission ahead. She thought he meant their current undercover job – not . . ." His eyes overflowed again, and he wiped the tears away.

Homer gulped hard. He'd never seen this side to his old friend. "Well, I need to get to the ER to see when they're releasing Mag. Let me know when you want our statements."

"I will. Thanks for everything you did to – to bring this case to closure, Homer. We'd be honored if you ever decide you want to come on the force. You'd be a real asset to the department. It's a given we want you to continue as a CI."

They shook hands, after they got across the street. Placing one hand on his friend's shoulder, he said, "Thanks, Len. I'll give it some thought, but I think I'll leave the cops and robbers game to you young squirts."

This brought a weak smile to Lenny Doan's face. He turned to walk to the bulletproof glass doors to enter the station, after they shook hands once again. Before going through them, he turned around to watch Homer get into his car. Damned fine undercover work, Wiley! Damned fine.

~ ~ ~

"Why don't you just spit it out?" Mag was still weak and pale. She'd fainted in the ER, so they moved her upstairs right away. Despite agreeing with Homer about her pallor and weakness, they released her after observing her overnight.

Carolyn tried to concentrate on the biography of a 19th century English woman by a local writer. She'd bought it at a book signing at Island Books the week before this thing started. It seemed like a year ago, but in truth, the first murder was committed just a little over a month ago. She sighed when she heard Maggie ask the question. It wasn't going to be easy for her to hear the answer.

Homer looked out beyond his deck. Egrets and pelicans were vying for food from the water and nearby banks. The scene was serene with emerald waters and robin egg blue sky as backdrops. It seemed nothing sinister could happen in that picture postcard world.

"Homer?"

He turned abruptly and looked at her. He still couldn't form the words.

"My God, what is it? Is this about what happened out there on the water last week?"

He swallowed the lump in his throat and cleared it a couple times. "Mag, 'Jake' – George Snow – he didn't make it."

Her hand flew to her mouth, and Carolyn rushed to her side. She stooped down and took her free hand, holding it tight, as Maggie cried.

"We're so sorry. All of us cared about him."

"She's right."

"But, who shot him? I saw the other man fall down in his boat."

"No one shot him, Mag." Carolyn didn't envy him in his task to tell her the truth. She remained silent.

"Did he fall overboard, too? Did he drown?"

"George shot himself and then he fell overboard."

"Oh dear God, that poor boy. He was so young."

"Yes, he was."

"Did they – did they get him back on board?"

"Yes, the chief and the lieutenant jumped in and got him, but it was too late. It looked like he died instantly."

"But, why did he shoot himself? Does anyone know? Of course, it was obvious he was involved or he'd not have tried to kill that man we'd been looking for, but I don't understand how he figured into it."

He took another deep breath. Carolyn refilled their coffee mugs and he shook his head in thanks. "You see, Strummond, as he called himself, was really an escaped convict."

"Then, it was him George was after, not Jackie or the trucker?"

"That's right."

"But, seems like he would have reported it to Lt. Butler or someone. You know, gotten backup to help him arrest someone who'd escaped from prison. It doesn't make sense he'd – kill him. Cops don't do that, do they?"

"No, usually they don't, not unless the perp is armed and shooting or threatening to kill the officer. In this case, Stummond probably never saw Snow until it was too late."

"But why?"

Homer sat down at the deck table and drank the rest of his coffee, trying to hold it together to get it all said, so she could deal with it, too, and put it behind her as they were trying to do. Carolyn touched his shoulder and he grasped her hand for a moment, before he spoke the awful words.

"Stummond – or Victor Marrow, his real name – raped and viciously killed George's young mother when the boy was just six years old."

"Oh dear God!" She made the sign of the cross, even though she wasn't Catholic. "He said she died a long time ago, not that he'd witnessed that horrible crime against her. Oh God, poor George."

"I'm – I'm afraid so, Mag. She hid him in the closet when Marrow was coming up the stairs. Told him to stay there and not to say a word, no matter what happened. There was no one else in the house, apparently. He didn't say anything about his father or any other man who might have been a father figure. Just said it was his mom and him."

"That poor little boy. No child should have to see something like that happen to his mother. No child!"

"Yeah, the poor guy described the scene to the chief. It sounded like the most gruesome crime anyone could witness. For her own little son to see all of it, I'm surprised it didn't make him go insane."

Carolyn touched his sleeve, gently, and said, "I think he did go a little insane when he finally confronted his mom's killer, don't you? Yes, he was a trained cop, but not trained to mutilate a criminal like that, unless he wasn't in his right mind when he did it."

He patted her hand, as he looked at Maggie. "Yeah, I expect you're close to the truth on that one. At least, temporary insanity while it was happening. I can't believe a great young cop like George Snow could plan and methodically carry out that kind of crime and still be of sound mind while he was doing it."

"My God," Maggie said, tears flowing down her cheeks. "My God."

Homer reached over and pulled her into his arms. "I'm so sorry. I hated to tell you the truth, but we couldn't hide the TV news and newspaper from you for much longer. We didn't want you to find out that way."

"I know." Her lips trembled and she moved her head back and forth several times. "I think I'm going to go in and take a nap. I thought I was stronger, but I'm pretty wiped out right now. Will you both excuse me, please?"

Carolyn hugged her. "Come on, Maggie. I'll take you in. We can have dinner later tonight."

Maggie tried to smile at her, but didn't quite make it. "I – I don't think I'll have any dinner tonight. You and Homer fix something you'd like – or better yet, why don't you go out to a nice place to eat. You saw an awful thing happen. That's a lot to go through."

Carolyn started to weep then, and pulled the other woman to her. "Oh God, it *was* horrible, yes, but you've been through a lot, yourself. You were so brave out there on the water. Everyone's calling you a hero, even the chief of police."

"That's just plain rubbish. I was closer than anyone else to him, that's all."

"You can play it down all you want, but you probably saved Lambert's life, and you nearly drowned in the process. Dear God, we thought we'd lost you."

"Well, you didn't and I'm fine."

"No, you're not. You need to regain your strength. Even if you don't feel up to eating a big meal, I'll bring you a small portion."

Maggie pressed her bony fingers down onto her friend's arm and patted it a few times. "Okay, I'll do it for you and Homer, but let me rest first. Okay?"

"Okay." She smiled and went over to draw the bamboo shades, after she pulled the afghan up over her. She watched for a few minutes, as the woman they all loved drifted off to what she hoped would be a peaceful sleep.

Homer was out on the deck when Carolyn came out of the guest room. "How is she?"

"She's going to be fine, Homer, but I expect she's going to blame herself for George's death for awhile."

"What? Why would she blame herself? She had nothing to do with his turning his weapon on himself."

She dropped into a seat at the table and took a sip of one of the bottles of Samuel Adams he'd opened for them. He joined her at the table, and continued to stare out to sea and the rapidly changing colors in the darkening sky. He never grew tired of that sunset, despite nearly forty years of playing the pipes at Mallory Square until sundown every night. He took one of the bottles and had a long drink before putting it down again.

Carolyn was watching the flaming sky, too. The bright red was fading to light purple, and the orange gave way to pastel yellow, as they watched. She took another sip of the beer, and then looked at Homer. "Probably because she couldn't get the gun away from him."

"That's nonsense! She nearly died, herself, when he pushed her and she slipped overboard. Why would she think such a thing?"

"She didn't come right out and say it, but I think she sees it as a failure on her part. As she said, she was the closest to him. She was the one trying to wrestle the gun from him."

"God, is this never going to end?"

"Eventually. Just give her time to go through it. Don't try to get her to block her feelings or she'll never heal."

He smiled at her, appreciating her quiet beauty. "When did you get so smart, luv?"

She smiled back, but didn't answer as she turned her head to watch the last semblance of colors fade from the darkening sky.

TWENTY

It was difficult to sit in the courtroom when Harry Bondare's trial started. Homer tried to get Maggie to stay home, but she insisted she was going to go with Carolyn and him.

She'd been back in her own home for six months, and had persuaded Carolyn, despite her dislike of Duval Street, to move in with her. She'd had the contractor come back to turn the third floor into a nice apartment with full kitchen for her friend and he was more than happy to come back, remembering the last time. Despite his protests, although he only had to do it one time, she still overpaid him by thousands. Carolyn found she loved living up there in her private space, where she had but to sit out on the wraparound porch to watch the lovely sunsets.

She still had the noisy tourists to contend with sometimes, but unless there was something special happening at the upper end of Duval, it was quiet compared to the lower end of the street where she'd lived before the murder of her neighbor. The residents closer to the Atlantic would not hear of the bars there staying open until the wee hours of the morning, so most of the owners set up shop elsewhere, leaving very few bars left at that end of the street. Since Carolyn lived on the third floor, she had unlimited visual access to the ocean, and sometimes she felt like she was back on Sugarloaf, especially after midnight when Duval and United were quiet. She was beginning to feel a quiet happiness envelope her since she moved into her new apartment.

*

The courtroom was hushed with tension, as the deputies brought the prisoner into it. Harry Bondare asked the defense to let him testify, saying he was going back to prison either way, so he had nothing to lose by telling the whole truth. His was the last testimony for the defense, and now the prosecution recalled him.

"Mr. Bondare, please tell this court why you agreed to help Detective Snow?"

"To begin with, I didn't know he was a cop. He just introduced himself as George Snow."

"And, did he approach you about murdering Mr. Drummond during that initial meeting?"

"Yes, he did. He told me the bas – sorry, your honor – Walter Drummond raped and murdered his mother when she was barely into her twenties. He said he was just six years old at the time. Said she hid him in her closet when she heard the stranger coming up the stairs."

"How did the idea of killing Mr. Weener and the trucker come up? Was that your idea or Detective Snow's?"

"Everything we did was the detective's idea. He masterminded the whole thing."

"But why Mr. Weener?"

"George said he wanted to take out a prominent figure in Key West, so all the attention of the cops would be on his death. That way, we could kill Strummond while they were all preoccupied with Weener's murder."

"Was there a particular reason he chose him over another prominent figure?"

"If there was he didn't tell me."

"Did you know Mr. Weener?"

"No, I didn't actually know him. Saw him around town a few times and I'd pass his shop every now and then."

"How about Fred Nouvel?"

"Who?"

"Fred Nouvel – you know, the trucker you killed."

"Oh. I never knew his name. No, I never saw him before."

'Then why did you kill him?"

"We had no choice. He saw us kill Jackie."

"Where did Mr. Weener's death take place? The mangroves?"

"No, we picked him up in Key West, threw him in the back of my truck, took him out to Card Sound Road and pulled off onto one of those little parking areas. It was real dark there, and very few cars that time of night, no trucks."

"There must have been at least one truck driving by, if you say you had to kill Mr. Nouvel because he saw what you did. Right?"

"I – yes, that's right. I meant besides him. The fool pulled off the road, and came back to my truck to see if we needed help. I'd forgotten to lock the door, and when he opened it, that's when he saw us. He started to run back to his truck, but Snow jumped out and grabbed him and – well, you know the rest."

The prosecutor tugged at his short goatee for a moment, as though in deep thought, and then he whirled back to stand in front of the defendant, with his face mere inches away. "Come on, Harry, tell the truth. Wasn't this whole thing your idea from the beginning?"

"No, I . . ."

"Wasn't it you who saw the opportunity to pick up where you left off before they caught you and sent you to prison for the murders of . . ."

Assistant Public Defender Joe Harden jumped to his feet. "Objection! Your honor, what the defendant did or didn't do years ago has no bearing on this case."

"Sustained."

Harden sat down, and continued taking notes. His client fidgeted in the witness chair, tugging on the tie he wasn't used to wearing.

"I'll rephrase the question, Mr. Bondare. Who was it who came up with the idea of killing the taxidermist and trucker?"

"George Snow."

"Did the detective know you'd been paroled from prison?"

"Yes, sir, when he told me he was a cop, he said he knew."

"Did he threaten you in any way to get you to help him?"

"Sure. Said if I didn't go along, he'd see I went back to prison for violating my parole."

"In what way were you violating your parole – before you killed those three people, that is?"

"I wasn't. I knew better than to carry, but he said he could make sure a weapon was found on me when the cops stopped me for that broken taillight."

"Did you have a broken tail light?"

"Not before he kicked it out."

"Objection!"

"Over-ruled. Go on, Mr. James."

"Thank you, your honor. Mr. Bondare, what is your real name?"

"Harry Bondare."

"How did you come up with the name Jeffrey Battles?"

The defendant swallowed and adjusted his tie again. Beads of sweat popped out on his forehead and around his mouth. He wiped his mouth with the sleeve of his dark blue jacket, leaving a visible dark stain trailing the length of it from his elbow.

"Mr. Bondare?"

"Jeffrey Battles was my brother-in-law," he croaked, almost in a whisper.

"Didn't you worry that he or your sister would object to your using his name?"

"I didn't give it any thought, sir."

"Mr. Bondare, are your sister and her husband, Jeffrey Battles, in this courtroom?"

"No," he whispered.

"Louder, Mr. Bondare. The jury can't hear you. Are your sister and her husband in this courtroom?"

"No."

"Why is that? Surely they wanted to support you during this difficult time?"

"They – they couldn't."

"And why is that, Mr. Bondare?"

Again, the defendant swiped at his mouth. "They – because, they're dead."

"How did they die, Harry?"

Bondare looked at the judge and then his eyes strayed to the jury. He half-stood and then slumped back down, but he didn't answer the question.

There was no sound in the courtroom, as the prosecutor waited patiently for his answer. Onlookers were leaning forward on the edge of their seats. Bondare looked more anxious as the minutes ticked by. He wondered why his lawyer didn't object to the question. He stared at the clock on the south wall of the room, his eyes following the swinging pendulum. He tugged at his shirt collar again. Wiped more sweat. Still silence prevailed in the large courtroom. Somewhere in the back someone stifled a cough.

"Mr. Bondare," the judge admonished him, "answer the question. Now."

The defendant breathed deeply, and then, without warning, he jumped up and ran toward a deputy, grabbing his weapon from its holster. People dove under their seats, afraid for their lives. Four other deputies were on him immediately, stopping him from pulling the trigger, as he turned the gun on himself. They cuffed him and snatched him from the courtroom.

"This court is adjourned until 9 tomorrow morning." The gavel came down. The black-robed Judge Applerouth disappeared behind the door to his chambers, after he dismissed the jury. Everyone stood, looking collectively astonished. Their murmurings sounded like a giant swarm of bees had just invaded the courtroom.

"My God, I can't believe that! He was going to kill himself," Maggie said, as Homer helped her to her feet and they turned to leave the courtroom.

"Yes, it looks that way. I'm sure glad he didn't. I, for one, couldn't take watching another man blow his brains out."

"That makes two of us," Homer told Carolyn.

"Will they put him on suicide watch, now?"

Homer looked at her for a moment, his expression unreadable. "I'm sure they will. As determined as he was just now, I'm sure if they didn't, he'd find a way to do it in his cell."

Maggie shivered. There'd been enough violence on their little island to last her remaining lifetime.

"Come on, let's get you ladies back home, and I'll fix us some sandwiches." He steered Maggie by her arm, as Carolyn walked the other side of her, guarding her through the crowd that was still standing in the courtroom.

"That sounds like just what the doctor ordered. I have a large container of turkey meat in the fridge and just bought some fresh romaine yesterday. After we eat, though, you two will have to go back up to Carolyn's. I'm exhausted and need to lie down for a good long nap."

Homer grinned at Carolyn over Maggie's head. She'd never give up trying to get them together. Not that he minded at all, but he knew Carolyn wanted no part of it.

Carolyn rolled her eyes, making him laugh. "I think the better idea is for you to go back to Sugarloaf after lunch, and for me to follow Maggie's lead and take a long nap, too. It's been a stressful and exhausting morning."

"Okay, I won't push it. Lunch and a nap for all of us, if that's how you want it to go down."

"It's the way I *want it to go down*." She smiled, but her eyes were determined. She looked at Maggie. "I think you should stay home tomorrow."

"No, I'm going back every day until that trial is over."

Homer frowned and helped her into the Hummer, after Carolyn climbed in ahead of her, into the back seat. "Okay, we won't force you to stay home. It could get rougher in the days ahead, though, so just be aware of that."

"If it gets too bad, I'll tell you to take me home. How's that?"

Smiling, her friend and chauffeur started the car, without further comment. Carolyn grinned at him through the rearview mirror, as she patted Maggie's hand, knowing she would never leave that courtroom for any reason, until it was over.

TWENTY-ONE

"Mr. Bondare, I want to remind you that you're still under oath," Judge Applerouth told him after he was seated.

"Yes, your honor."

The judge looked at the prosecutor. "Mr. James?"

The assistant state attorney left his seat and went to stand in front of the defendant. "Good morning, Mr. Bondare. Are you feeling better today?"

The startled man looked puzzled, but told him he was feeling all right.

"Before court adjourned yesterday, you were about to answer my question. Do you remember what it was?"

"No sir."

"I'll repeat it for you. How did your sister and her husband die?"

The defendant, who was restrained to the large leather chair this time to avoid another attempt at suicide, turned as pale as blackboard chalk. He was a deer caught in the headlights, and once again, sweat popped out on his forehead. His eyes drifted to the jury, who like the rest of the onlookers, were leaning toward him to hear his answer. As he had the day before, he leaned his head over and wiped the sweat with his jacket sleeve.

"We're all waiting, Mr. Bondare."

"Okay – okay!" His voice was almost a scream.

The young assistant state attorney pretended to be puzzled. "Okay what?"

"Okay, I killed them!" he shouted. "There, are all of you happy now?"

Multiple gasps were heard throughout the room.

"You killed both of them?"

"Yeah, they've been dead almost a year."

"Why did you kill your own sister and her husband?"

"I was staying with them after I got out of prison. Things were going pretty good, but then I lost my job. Jeff kept complaining to Kate about me being a moocher, not holding up my end, ya know."

"So, that's why you killed him?"

"Yeah, wouldn't you have?"

"Objection. Your honor, I need a moment with my client."

"Approach."

Both attorneys went to the bench. Covering his microphone, the judge said, "I'm allowing this testimony, Mr. Harden. Your client has already volunteered that he committed two more cold-blooded homicides, so I don't want you to tell him not to continue. You had your chance earlier. Please return to your seat. You may continue, Mr. James."

"But, your honor . . ."

"Now, Mr. Harden."

The ASA resumed the line of questioning. "Something puzzles me, Mr. Bondare. Why do your sister in, if it was your brother-in-law doing the complaining?"

"She went along with him. Asked – no, the bitch *ordered* me to leave."

"I see. How did you kill them? With a gun?"

"No, I told you I don't carry. Didn't want to go back to prison." Someone giggled in the back of the courtroom. The judge brought the gavel down and once more silence prevailed.

"How then?"

"I – I slipped into their bedroom the night before I was supposed to get out. The lights were out and they looked like they were sound asleep."

"And were they?"

"He was, but Sis wasn't quite there, yet."

"So, she saw you come into the room?"

"Yeah."

"What did she say?"

"She didn't say nothin. Just screamed."

"Why did she scream? For all she knew, you just needed to tell them something before you left in the morning."

"She screamed 'cause she saw her largest butcher knife in my hand."

"Did that wake her husband up?"

"Yeah, he was sort of in a fog at first, and then he saw me. Lunged at me across the bed and tried to get the knife out of my hand."

"What happened then?"

"I hit him with the bedside lamp, and he fell against the headboard. I guess it just stunned him, 'cause he started to get up, but I walked to that side of the bed and slit his throat before he could manage it."

"What was your sister doing all this time?"

"I guess she went into shock, 'cause she just sat there in bed and watched."

"She just watched? She was no longer screaming?"

"No."

"Did she call 911?"

"Nope." He grinned and stared at the ASA, daring him to continue the line of questioning.

The prosecutor ignored his goading. "If she was in shock and not calling for help, why didn't you just leave? Why kill her?"

"She finally snapped out of it and called me a crazy animal. Said I was fu – frigging insane."

"What did you do when she said that?"

"I lost it, of course. I went back to her side of the bed, grabbed her by the hair and slit *her* throat."

Charlie James turned, facing the jurors. "And then you left." It was not a question.

"No, I stayed for awhile."

"To clean up the mess, the blood?"

145

"That happened after."

The prosecutor turned around to face him again. "After?"

"Yeah, after I cut them up. Cut their hands and legs off, and stuffed them into large trash bags." Gasps fluttered through the courtroom. One woman on the jury fainted. While the bailiff was tending to her, another woman, a spectator, gagged and rushed out of the courtroom.

"Objection!"

"Overruled." Seeing that the woman on the jury was seated again, and she had assured him she was all right, he added, "You may proceed, Mr. James."

"Where did you put those trash bags, Mr. Bondare?"

"I hauled them out to my truck – actually my brother-in-law's truck, started the engine and just started driving. Buried them a hundred miles from there, in a Georgia state forest."

"Were they ever found?"

"Not to my knowledge – never heard about it, if they were."

"Where did you go after that?"

"I went back to the house, to clean it up and make it into a home, again. Couldn't live in such a mess, could I?" He licked his lips and then smiled at the prosecutor. "I stayed there for several months, before I moved to the Keys."

"How did you manage to live and pay the mortgage?"

"I used Jeff's Social Security checks, of course, and then I notified the Social Security office that I'd moved, so they could continue to send them to me." He smiled at the jury again, and was met with looks of disgust.

With his back to the defendant, and staring at the jury, James said, "So, you left your sister and brother-in-law in the same condition as you and Detective Snow left Mr. Weener, Mr. Nouvel and Mr. Strummond."

"Objection – the prosecutor is testifying."

"Sustained."

"I'll refrain the question, your honor. Whose idea was it to mutilate the bodies of Mr. Weener, Mr. Nouvel and Mr. Strummond?"

"Uh – I told Snow it would be better to – to cut off body parts, so they couldn't be identified." Again, he stared smugly at the jury.

"But, they were easily identified, weren't they – you even left Mr. Strummond in his own condo, didn't you?"

"Yes, that was the detective's idea."

"The detective's?"

"Yeah – Snow. It was his idea. He went along with the mutilation to an extent. Said he wanted to go further and make it look like – you know – sex killings. To throw the cops off and make them think they were crimes of – of – oh, you know - whatchamacallit – uh, passion. Yeah, that's it. Crimes of passion. By a jealous husband or something like that, he said. I thought that was friggin' brilliant, even if he did think of it first."

"So, cutting off the sex organs was all Snow contributed to the plan, besides engaging in the killing with you?"

"That's right." He smiled at the prosecutor and then his eyes roamed once more over the members of the jury, who still were looking at him in disgust and disbelief. "I was the one who thought of stuffing them in their mouths."

James looked at the jury in time to see the woman who'd fainted turn white. Afraid she'd faint again, he addressed the judge.

"Your honor, is she all right?" He inclined his head to the jury box.

"I was wondering that myself, young man. Ma'am, do you want to be excused? We can use the alternate juror for the rest of the trial, if you're too ill to continue."

She shook her head, stood and started to say she was all right, but fainted again, instead. Two of the male jurors caught her before she fell to the floor. "Deputy," he said, addressing the nearest female officer, "please help the bailiff get her to the jury room and stay with her until the doctor clears her to leave. Bailiff, please call Dr. Olson as soon as you get to the jury room, and ask him to come over as soon as possible."

The female deputy and the bailiff did as he instructed, and soon the courtroom was quiet again.

"Will juror number thirteen please come to the jury box?"

After the juror, who'd been seated in the courtroom as instructed, was seated in the jury box and given further instructions by the judge,

Applerouth nodded to the prosecutor to resume his questioning. "Thank you for your patience, Mr. James. You may proceed."

"Thank you, your honor. Tell me, Mr. Bondare, if you can, what was Detective Snow's state of mind while he was helping you kill Mr. Strummond?"

"Objection! Calls for credentials the witness does not have, your honor."

"Sustained. Rephrase your question, Mr. James," the judge said in a weary tone.

"Yes, your honor. Mr. Bondare, was Detective Snow smiling while he was killing the victim?"

"Are you friggin' kidding me? He didn't have the balls for that. Naw, he was bawlin' like a baby the whole time. Never saw nothin' like it."

"Did he say anything to Mr. Strummond while he was helping you kill him?"

"Yeah, I think he said, 'this is for Mom, you sonofabitch.'"

"At that point, was Mr. Strummond able to speak?"

"Yeah, he hadn't slit his throat yet, 'cause he said he didn't want him to die fast. He wanted him to feel us cutting off his limbs – and other parts." There were a few coughs and clearing of throats in the courtroom. The prosecutor waited until everyone was quiet again.

"What did he say to Detective Snow, if anything?'

"He asked him who he was."

"Did he answer?"

"Yeah, that was the only time he smiled. He said, 'I'm Jessica Snow's son. I was hiding in the closet when you butchered her, you sonofabitch.'"

"What was the victim's reaction?"

"His mouth flew open, but he didn't get to say anything, 'cause Snow cut his throat before he could. I thought he was gonna decapitate him, but then he stopped."

"So he didn't do any of the other mutilation on him?"

"Oh yeah. He was still bawling, though, and once he looked at me and said, 'Mom wouldn't approve, but I can't fail her again.' I thought that was kinda weird, since he was only six when it happened. Don't know what he thought he coulda done to stop it."

"What about when he helped you kill Mr. Weener and Mr. Nouvel? Was he crying then?"

"No, he kept telling Mr. Weener he was sorry. And he didn't say anything to the trucker. That I heard, anyway."

"You said he kept telling Mr. Weener he was sorry. Was that before he slashed his throat or after?"

"No, that was later."

"What happened before he slashed his throat?"

"Snow didn't want anything to happen while he was alive, but I'd already started, so I cut off his hands and feet while he was ponderin' whether to slash his throat."

"While he was alive?"

"Didn't I just say that?"

"No, I don't think you were clear about that."

"Sorry, thought you understood me." He shrugged and again looked at the jury and smiled. Their glares caused him to turn back to the prosecutor, who was glaring, also.

"No further questions, your honor."

"Mr. Harden?"

The public defender didn't raise his head. "No questions, your honor."

"What?" Bondare looked surprised. "But, you have to question me. You're my friggin' lawyer!"

"Silence!" The gavel came down again. "The defendant may step down." Two deputies aided him, because of his body restraint.

"The prosecution rests, your honor."

"This court is adjourned until tomorrow at 9. Gentlemen, we'll have your summations at that time."

After the gavel came down, the jury was taken back to the Doubletree where they'd been sequestered since the beginning of the trial, after being reminded by the judge not to read or listen to anything dealing with the case and not to discuss the case amongst themselves, which of course they did all through dinner.

"Well, that was mind-blowing," Homer told his companions. "Unbelievable!"

"You can say that again." Maggie looked more peaked than the day before, but she insisted they all go out to lunch, since it was still early.

After they were seated oceanside at Louie's Backyard, Carolyn asked, "Do you think the police will go to that forest to look for the bodies of his relatives?"

"I heard Lenny Doan on the phone to the FBI outside in the hallway after we left the courtroom," Homer told her. "Since they were butchered outside Tallahassee and then buried out of state, the feds will have to take care of that. God, those poor people!"

"That Bondare fella is some kind of fiend, isn't he? Who kills his own sister like that?"

"You just said it, Mag. A fiend. I'm wondering whether his attorney is going to try to get him an insanity plea."

"Isn't it too late for that?"

"I'm not sure, to tell the truth. I think it depends upon whether he can get the prosecution to go along with it at this stage of the trial. Otherwise, it's essentially over, and after their closing arguments in the morning, it'll go to the jury. Of course, there has to be a pre-sentence investigation. Who knows, the psychiatrists might come back and say he's insane."

Maggie shivered, despite the heat. "Let's eat our nice lunch and forget about this for awhile. What do you say?"

They both agreed, and started eating, although none of the three felt much like it. Or really tasted the food put before them. Looking out at the tranquil sea, their collective minds were filled with the ghastly details of the five crimes that had been described on the stand by not only the medical examiner in the case of the three local murders, but by the defendant's gleefully describing the murders he committed before linking up with the young and troubled detective. The murders he would have to stand trial for after this one was finished, regardless of the jury's verdict.

TWENTY-TWO

There was no plea offered, and the jury took just two hours to render their verdict – guilty of three counts kidnapping and one count second-degree murder of the trucker and two counts first-degree murder of the taxidermist and Strummond.

A pre-sentence psych eval determined the defendant to be of sound mind when he helped commit the murders, so he was sentenced to life in prison with no chance of parole this time. Having him stand trial for the murders of his sister and brother-in-law in Tallahassee where the murders were committed seemed to Homer anti-climactic, but it was necessary. "I expect he'll get the death penalty for those," he told his female companions.

"He looked like pure evil on that witness stand."

He looked at Carolyn and then said, "That was my thought, exactly, as I watched and listened to him."

"If the truth were known, I suspect he took advantage of poor George's state of mind after years of heartache and bitterness over what Strummond did to his mother," Maggie said to them.

"I wouldn't doubt that one bit. But, then, because George killed himself, we'll never know the whole story," he added.

"Poor George," Maggie repeated, with tears in her eyes. She'd come to care for him like a son during those two months of seclusion with him and Ken Lambert, while the others were in Cuba searching for the killer, never suspecting it was one of their own. Never suspecting it was him. Soon, her tears turned to outright sobbing, and her friends let her have her cry, as they each laid a hand on an arm to console her. They'd never seen their Maggie cry before, much less uncontrollably like this and they looked at each other in helplessness.

The talk in Key West was about nothing but the murders and trial for months following, but gradually things returned to normal for the locals, including Maggie, who treated the other two to a trip back to Cuba. "This is going to be fun, Homer. We've never been over there together, you know."

He smiled. "Yes, I know. And, I'll go on one condition, Mag."

"What's that?"

"That you don't try to smuggle any contraband, not even one sheet of paper, out of Cuba."

"But, that's the fun of . . ."

"No, not a single item, unless you want me to stay home. And, trust me, I'll try to persuade Carolyn not to go, too, if you don't promise."

Looking out to sea, where a couple of dolphins were flip-flopping repeatedly into the air, she was silent. She loved the show they put on for the humans. She could only see it from Carolyn's porch, where the three were sitting now, and enjoying late afternoon tea.

"Mag?"

"Oh, okay, I promise I won't bring a thing back."

He sighed with relief. "Okay, then, let's start packing. When do you want to go?"

"Can you try to get us on a plane out of MIA tomorrow?"

"Wow – you really are eager to get out of here, aren't you?"

"We need it, Homer."

He shrugged. "Okay, we'll be ready tomorrow."

"Do you want me to call the airlines?"

"No, thanks," he told Carolyn. "I'll do it. I'll see you both at dinnertime. I'm taking us out to eat, by the way."

Maggie and Carolyn smiled at him. Neither was in the mood to cook a meal. He walked downstairs, and they heard the front door close behind him. They continued to sit in silence, watching the tableau unfolding in the sea and the sky, as the sunset approached in vivid reds and yellows. "We're lucky women, Carolyn." Her friend agreed with a nod of her head. "He's been a great friend to me since the day we met. He doesn't open that door to too many people, and now, he's opened it to you, too."

"Yes, he's become a good friend, just as you have, and I'm grateful for that, after all that's happened. The murder in my building on the heels of the divorce, and then realizing that someone who was living with us and keeping us safe from the killer actually was one of the killers. And worst of all, having to watch him shoot himself like that and die before my eyes."

"I'm glad I didn't see it. I'm sure it's a lot to process just when you were trying to put your life back together."

"Did you think it was odd that George got such a send-off from the police department?"

Maggie looked at her, and then shrugged her shoulders. "Not really. He did a horrible thing, but he was a good cop before that. I think they were just trying to honor his being a brother, and to forget for those few moments what he did to dishonor the badge."

"I suppose you're right. It just seems the one would overshadow what came before. Honestly, I wonder what the chief was thinking by having that kind of service for someone who dishonored the department."

"I talked to Lenny Doan about it the other day."

Surprised, Carolyn looked over at her. "Oh?"

"Yes. He was looking really down when he walked past the house, so I called him up to have a cold lemonade with me on the porch. I came right out and asked why they gave him the honorable send-off."

"And?"

She smiled at her friend. "At first, he just chalked it up to this being Key West. And then, he said it was far less than they would have given him had he died in the line of duty under different circumstances. He said if he hadn't killed those men, he'd have had a full and honorable funeral, possession through town to the cemetery and a full-gun salute at the gravesite. If you recall, all they did was play taps after they shot a volley into the air before he was interred."

153

"But, it looked like every cop in town was at the gravesite, Mag."

"Yes, but they were there because they wanted to be. The chief said, under the circumstances, he didn't make attendance mandatory for anyone."

"Oh? It sure looked like it."

"As he said, that was a testament to how well-liked George was by all the others in the department."

"I wonder, though, how they could put the rest behind them."

"The chief said when they learned what he'd seen happen to his mother at the age of six, they wanted to try to forget the horror of his last months on this earth and just remember him for the good cop he'd been. The whole department attended group counseling for a while, after his death."

"That's understandable."

"Yes, and Lenny confided that he didn't know how he'd have reacted to finding his mother's killer, had he been in Snow's shoes. He said he had a feeling he'd have wanted to take his own retribution against the guy, too, instead of letting the law handle it. That he probably would have gone stark raving mad when he saw him again, as George probably did in that first awful moment of recognition."

Carolyn shivered, though the evening was still sultry. "I wondered about that. Does anyone know when he first saw him again?"

"The chief said he wanted to know the answer to that, too, but felt the important thing was to try to talk George down so they could get him some help. Of course, it was too late to reach him by that time. He was determined to end his life rather than go to prison, if he wasn't allowed to simply disappear, as he begged of the chief."

"I'm sure it would take almost superhuman strength not to want to exact vengeance if one saw the killer of a loved one. I doubt I'd be that strong, either," Carolyn said.

"If I'd seen a man walking around free after killing my mother, I'd go crazy with fury and want to avenge her right there and then."

The other woman smiled at her, reached over and patted her hand. "Ms. Maggie, I can't imagine you could hurt anyone, much less kill him, even for that reason."

"You'd be surprised then."

"Is that why you wanted to do it so badly?"

"Honor George by attending the service, you mean?" Her lips were trembling and her voice was a whisper. Carolyn nodded her head and got a weak, "Yes."

She'd never seen her this raw emotionally except for that afternoon at the restaurant when she was sobbing. "I'm glad we went," she told her friend.

"He was a good cop and good to us when Homer was in Cuba. That made it easy to push everything else aside. It was obvious he was a tortured soul at the end. Oh I'm not saying it's easy to forget the heinous murders he committed, but somehow it doesn't overshadow the goodness in him aside from that."

Carolyn looked thoughtful and said, "You could have died when he pushed you overboard. Don't you even have bad feelings toward him over that?"

"Is that what everyone thinks? But, Carolyn, he didn't push me overboard. He pushed me away from him when I was trying to get the gun. That's all. He could have shot me, but he didn't. I just happened to lose my balance and fall into the water when he kicked me away from him. He wasn't trying to hurt me. He pleaded with me to stand back."

"I didn't know that. It was hard to see and hear exactly what was happening. You jumped him so suddenly, it took us all by surprise." She looked at Maggie in awe. "I couldn't have been that brave with him having that weapon on us."

"Bravery had nothing to do with it, my friend."

Carolyn smiled at her. She didn't believe that for a moment. "Well, while Homer's making our reservations, I'm going to take a little nap before I pack for our trip."

"Sounds like a good idea. Think I'll do the same. See you after while." The women stood and hugged for a brief moment, saying nothing more. Maggie walked through the apartment to take the stairs to the second floor. When she got there, she went into her bedroom and lay on her bed for a long time. Her mind wouldn't shut down, as she stared at the gigantic ficus tree beyond the French doors to her deck. Finally, her eyes closed and she slept soundly for two hours, until she heard the front door open and Homer walk into the foyer below her room.

TWENTY-THREE

It was even hotter when the three of them got off the plane that took them from Cancun to Cuba, but strong trade winds caressed them, diluting the sultry air. Despite the obvious poverty abounding in the form of the shack-like homes and businesses around them, everything seemed to be a deeper shade of green than any tree or plant in Key West, as beautiful as that small island was. Beautiful flowers were everywhere they looked. Even the Caribbean Sea seemed a deeper blue than the Atlantic or the Gulf, despite its running into both of them. "It's beautiful, Homer! Somehow I didn't think it would be. It must be because of all the mountains surrounding it."

He grinned at Carolyn and got a big smile in return. "We told you, didn't we?"

"Yes, you did. I have a feeling this big island is just what the doctor ordered."

"It always is for me," Maggie told her, her toothless smile wide. "I hate it when I have to leave."

"Yeah, right! Tell the truth; you can't wait to get back to sell all your contraband." He laughed when she made a face, causing Carolyn to join him in the most laughter they'd heard from her in months. Maggie shrugged, turned her back to them and started walking toward their *casa particular*, which they could see in the distance.

Carolyn agreed to stay in one after they both described the difference between them and the local hotels. The owner of the large one Homer always stayed in was able to rent them three rooms, with a bath between two of them. Homer said he'd take the far room, and they could have the other two. That way he wouldn't have to walk through one of their rooms to get to the bathroom. He'd explained before they left Cancun that the little village they were going to had no 4 or 5-star hotels, but if she wanted one of them, they could stay in the city.

"No, I want to experience the real Cuba, the one you and Mag seem to know so well. I doubt I'd find that in Havana. By the way, Shirley was telling me about the sweet Cuban woman and her grandchildren whom you help on a regular basis. Hope I get to meet them."

"Shirley has a big mouth."

"Oh come on, Homer. We all know you're a good person, so don't try to downplay your benevolence to us."

Ignoring that, he said, "We'd better push ahead before we lose our rooms." Maggie was already almost a block ahead of them.

She laughed. "Looks like Mag will make sure that doesn't happen."

"She's sure in a big hurry for some reason. She never walks that fast." Then, it dawned on him and he hit his forehead with the flat of his hand. "Dammit! I'll bet she's already called someone to arrange to buy something she shouldn't. Let's catch up with her. We can't afford to land in jail over here. If she thinks jail in Key West is bad, she has no idea how unpleasant it is over here."

Carolyn grinned. "Had a little experience with that, eh?"

"No, I – oh all right, yeah, they've thrown me in lockup once or twice."

"Once or twice?" Her eyebrows went up. "What on earth did you do?"

"Those were my younger days, and I got a little too drunk a couple times too many. Bothered the wrong woman and felt the fists and boots of her man."

"The same woman both times?"

"No, two different women, with two different and very tough boyfriends," he said, laughing. "That was before I joined the Marines."

She giggled. "Please, try to stay out of trouble this time. I don't want to be the only one they allow to go home."

He laughed again. "Wouldn't dream of leaving you stranded."

"Hey Mag, what's the rush?" They were winded, but they'd caught up to her.

"Rush? What rush?"

"You've been at least a block ahead of us since you got off the plane. You have an appointment with someone?"

She gave him a look that made both of them stifle giggles. "With whom would I have an appointment? I don't know everyone on the island like you do, Homer, after telling me all these years you'd never been here before."

"Ha! Don't give me that. You know half of Cuba." He threw an arm over her bony shoulder. "You can't deny that. Everyone you passed said *hola* to you."

"That's not true and you know it." He was teasing, but after what they'd been through, she'd give him that.

"Well, maybe it was a little bit of an exaggeration, but there were two or three who seemed to know you pretty darn well."

"Maybe one or two."

"Okay," he said, laughing loudly.

Just then three young men passed and said at once, "*Hola, Senorita Maggie.*" She smiled and said hello back to them.

Homer looked at her, and then to Carolyn, spreading his hands. "I rest my case!" She laughed, but Maggie just said something under her breath to Homer, causing Carolyn to laugh harder.

"Don't look at me. You should have warned them not to speak to you."

"Harrumph!" She gave him the eagle eye again, producing yet another giggle from Carolyn, who said, "I don't think I ever enjoyed life this much before I met the two of you. I was just a bitter middle-aged woman before we got together. I sure don't remember laughing as much! Barring the unpleasant situation we just lived through, that is."

Homer grinned, but didn't comment. To Maggie, she asked, "Do you enjoy the *casa particular* more than a hotel, Maggie?"

"Oh sure. They treat us Americans like we're God's gift to Cuba. They think we're all rich," she added, not that she wasn't.

"Yeah, especially if we tip big." He and Carolyn laughed again. Her habit of just reaching into her pocket and giving the person every bill in it was never lost on them.

"Well, if it makes me happy to be generous with my own money, what does it hurt anyone else?"

Putting an arm around her, Carolyn agreed, "It doesn't hurt a thing, darlin'. You're a good soul for doing it."

"Harrumph," she mumbled again.

~ ~ ~

"Mama – Carmelita, this is Carolyn and this is Maggie. You've heard me talk about her for a long time," he told the weary-looking grandmother in Spanish.

"About time you brought her," she replied in Spanish. "*Hola*, Maggie. *Hola*, Carolyn."

"*Hola*, Carmelita. It's nice to meet you," they both told her.

Homer translated, and she told them the same.

"Homer, do you think she'd mind if I gave her a little extra on top of what you give her?"

He laughed and said, "She'll probably be the richest woman on the island if you do that, but I'm sure she won't mind. She has a license to sell her *cajitas*, but most of the time, she barely scrapes by in this old shack. I'll tell her we'll put most of it into the savings account I set up for them."

"Okay, then, here's a little to help out." She reached into her pocket and instead of pulling out a couple hundred, she handed him two thousand.

When Homer told the older woman how much Maggie was giving her, her face turned as white as alabaster and she swayed, as though about to faint. Carolyn hurried to her, and had her take a sip of the *café con leche* she'd been nursing as they walked up.

Soon the old woman smiled and Maggie returned it with her big toothless smile, which wasn't that unusual around this little country village. Carmelita, herself, had very few teeth in her head. Homer had offered to pay for a dentist in Havana or bring her over to the states to see Dr. Troxel, but she refused, saying she'd managed all these years without teeth, and was fine with it.

With tears in her big brown eyes, Carmelita told her, "*Muchas gracias, Senorita* Maggie, *muchas gracias*," over and over.

"*Da nada*," Maggie told her, shrugging it off. "Homer, tell her it was nothing; I was glad to help."

"Don't think she'll believe it was nothing, Mag, but I'll tell her. Do you know that what you gave her is about what most people earn in a year over here?"

"Oh my God, that's horrible."

TWENTY-FOUR

After Homer relayed Maggie's message to her, and they were assured she was all right, they bid her goodbye, and walked toward the plaza. Maggie repeated her dismay over the small amount of wages workers in Cuba earned, and Homer shrugged.

"I can't agree more, but don't see it changing until we lift that damned embargo and Castro decides to give the people a little of that democracy they crave. But, most will tell you that will happen only in their dreams. They've given up on its ever being any different. I'm sure they're right."

"They should never give up, Homer. Things will change one day; I know it. I think Obama will get that embargo lifted in his second term, and then you'll see things getting better for these people."

He cringed. "God forbid he gets a second term. But, yeah, he'll lift it, just like every other Democrat has lifted it." Maggie ignored his admonishment of the Democratic president, as she always did. She voted for President Barack Obama and she'd do it again, if he ran for another term.

"Despite the financial hardship on them, they seem to be a happy people," Carolyn said.

"Yes, for the most part, they are. The Cubans are great at making lemonade out of lemons," he told her. "They don't sit around brooding when things don't go their way, like too many of us Americans are prone to do. They love to laugh and love to dance. That's one thing Castro could never take away from them. You'll see tonight after the sun goes down. You think there's a lot of music in the air, now, just wait. You'll hear music and see dancing everywhere all night long."

"Is it that way just in and near Havana, or the same everywhere on the island?"

"Naturally being the capital, Havana is where it's at as far as the nightlife goes, but it's pretty much the same everywhere you go here," he told her.

"Wait till you see some of the parks in Cuba. Some of them rival our best national parks," Maggie added.

Homer joined in on that subject. "We'll go to *Pinar del Rio* this evening and I'll take you to *Vinales* before we leave. It's one of the best national parks, where most of the tourists go who want to hike the mountains and explore the caves."

"That sounds peaceful."

"It is. You'll enjoy it." He looked at Maggie. "Don't know how much you're going to be up for, but we'll take it easy on you."

"What? When have you ever had to cater to me? I can keep up with you young whippersnappers any old day, and you darn well know it."

They smiled and then Homer turned the corner, and opened the door of the *Banco Metropolitano* branch. "It'll take me just a few minutes to deposit Carmelita's money into her savings account. Then, I think we'd better have a siesta. It doesn't do to walk around in this afternoon heat."

"Sounds good to me."

"Me, too," Maggie told them.

"What happened to keeping up with us whippersnappers?" Homer teased.

"What you do, I do," was her staid reply.

He'd taken them to the airport's visa office as soon as they arrived, explaining to Carolyn that their tourist visas would be valid only for 30 days, but if they decided they wanted to stay longer, it could be extended for another 30 days at the immigration office.

"Let's play it by ear," she told him. "We might want to leave after a couple or three weeks."

"Okay, sounds good to me. We can also leave after the 30-day extension, for anywhere we want to go, and then come back into Cuba on another two-month visa. We can only do that once, though."

"That sounds pretty lenient for a Communist country."

"Yes, it's a pretty good deal. Even though they want to keep control by setting up these little rules, they like our money too much to keep us out entirely."

He went into the bank and deposited the money. When he walked back outside, he suggested they take the *Astro* back to their *casa*.

"*Astro?*"

"Oh, forgot you haven't been here before. It's one of the bus lines, and the best way to get around, unless you rent a scooter, which we won't do this trip."

"Good. You scare me to death in Key West on your scooter. Sure don't want to ride one over here on these rutty roads."

He laughed. "Woman, you need to take more risks."

"I enjoy staying alive too much," she said, as she, too, laughed about it. Homer took her on one ride through the streets of Key West after a city commission meeting, and she thought any moment she'd lose an arm or leg, because he got so close to other vehicles or to the light poles on the sidewalks, when he suddenly veered up onto them to take a short cut. After they arrived at their destination, she told him she'd walk home, and she did.

He grinned, knowing what she was thinking. Maggie was silent throughout their bantering discussion that was continued on the bus. It was loaded with mostly Cubans, some chattering with excitement, some singing and playing guitars, while others were pensive and stared out at the countryside as the bus drove them to their homes for siesta. He explained that tourists usually take the *Viazul* line. "It's air-conditioned and has a washroom, and TVs, since it travels long-distance." Most Cubans took the *Astro*, and because he was fluent in the language, he always took it, too. He had come over so often, he'd not felt like a tourist in many years, nor was he treated like one by the Cubans who knew him.

"You okay, Mag?"

"Oh sure, just a little sleepy." She looked too pale to Carolyn. Homer didn't mention it, but he thought she did, also.

Carolyn put her arm around their older companion, and they walked behind Homer, after they got off the bus. "We'll be back soon and you can lie down. I'm ready for that siesta, too."

Each of them slept for nearly three hours, awakening to a darkened room. When they'd splashed water on their faces, and changed, they met outside on the veranda. He smiled when he saw the ladies walking toward him. "Guess it's a little too late to go to the park, ladies, but we can go to the *paladares* for a fair meal and Cuban coffee cocktails."

Carolyn made a face. "Somehow that doesn't appeal to me, Homer."

"You'll love it. It's made with a little Coconut rum, a little dark *crème de Coco* and good strong Cuban *café*. They top the whole thing with whipped cream, and I'll guarantee it's delicious."

"Is that what you drink the whole time you're over here?"

"Nah, I drink *café con leche* most of the time when I'm not drinking *Cristal*."

"*Cristal* coffee? What's that?"

He laughed. "No, *Cristal's* a beer."

"Oh. Well, I'm willing to try that coffee cocktail at least once. Are you having it?" She looked at Maggie and was pleased that she wasn't so pale after her nap.

"Wouldn't miss it. I only have it once a night, though. It's pretty strong. Most of the time, like Homer, I drink just *café con leche* or beer. The *Cristal* is too strong for me, though. I like the *Bucanero* better, although sometimes it's harder to find than *Cristal*, which is everywhere, like *Red Stripe* in Jamaica."

"Here we are, ladies. Looks like we're just in time. Pretty soon they'll start turning people away."

"Why would they do that?"

"Just not enough room to seat everyone, so you always have to get here early to get a seat and a meal."

"The food must be great then."

"Here it is, yes."

"Are these the only places besides the hotels where tourists can eat?"

"No, sometimes, if you're willing to pay in what they call *CUCs*, which are convertible *pesos*, you can eat in state-run restaurants and get better food. The food in this place runs a close second, though, and is much cheaper."

"Well, if nothing else, I'm getting an education coming here with the two of you world-travelers."

They smiled, and Maggie said, "He's the world-traveler. I only go between Mexico and Cuba, once in a while to Jamaica."

After they had been seated for a while, a stern-looking Cuban man came over to their table. "*Hola, Senorita* Maggie."

"Uh – *hola, Senor* Perez."

"Got a lot of good stuff," he said in English, his handlebar black mustache turning up with his broad smile. "Wanna see some of it, now?"

Maggie looked at him, then at Homer, who was daring her with his eyes. "Uh, perhaps another time. My friends and I are on vacation, so I probably won't bother with it this trip. You understand."

The man looked puzzled, but quickly caught on, especially after he saw the glare in Homer's eyes. "Oh, of course, *Senorita*. Maybe next time." He tipped his hat to her and then to Homer and Carolyn. "Enjoy your holiday."

After he was gone, she looked at Homer and said, "Not a word."

He shrugged and took another big sip of his coffee cocktail, as Carolyn hid a grin behind her cup.

TWENTY-FIVE

"It's good to be home." Carolyn brought their plates of shrimp Creole to Maggie's small round table in the kitchen. She'd offered to do dinner, and had been cooking since they walked in the door and she'd taken her things upstairs. She'd changed into shorts and a light cotton shirt before she came back down.

"Amen to that!" Maggie took a big scoop of the shrimp Creole onto her plate, after she finished her salad. "And to tell the truth, I'm glad we only stayed two weeks."

"I am, too, Mag. It was nice to finally go there, but after two weeks of any new place, I'm ready for the comfort of home."

"I have to agree with you ladies. It's good to be home. Sorry you had to come back empty-handed, Mag, but we'd been in enough trouble before everything got resolved over here. We didn't need for Customs to catch us trying to smuggle anything into the country." He smiled at her, and got a small one in return. He wished he could see the old Maggie again. She'd not been the same since George's death.

"Don't worry about it. I really wasn't up for buying anything this trip." They looked at her with concern.

"Were you not feeling well over there?" Carolyn asked, after swallowing a large shrimp.

"Sure, I wouldn't have run around the island if I hadn't been. After what we'd all been through, it just didn't seem that important to me. Maybe it never will again." She looked at Homer, who smiled broadly. He hoped she'd stick to that. She knew he'd never approved of her bringing back any of the treasures she'd found over there on the black market, but she'd sure enjoyed doing it.

"This Creole is delicious," Homer said. "I might just marry you if you cook like this all the time." He winked at Carolyn who shot him a sharp look. He laughed, but said no more.

After a half slice of Key lime pie, Maggie yawned and said, "I don't know about the two of you, but even though it's only eight-thirty, this old gal is ready to call it a night."

The other two agreed with her, Homer left after giving them both a peck on the cheek, and Carolyn went up to her apartment. They all slept without awakening, as none of them had done since the first murder victim was found on Card Sound, and by eight the next morning, they were ready to tackle anything that needed done.

After lunch, Homer called Carolyn. "It's about Maggie."

"Oh? What's going on, Homer? Oh dear Lord, she's sick?"

"No, it's nothing like that. Mag's fine. I just want to do something she isn't going to like and I need your help."

"Oh boy, I don't think I like the sound of that. It sounds too much like something Maggie would say, and that never led to anything but trouble."

After he finished explaining, he asked, "Will you back me on it, please?"

"Sure, I'd like that as much as you would. She really deserves it."

~ ~ ~

He leaned closer. "Do you think she suspects anything?"

"If she does, she's keeping it to herself. She was reluctant to go for another drive, but that's all she said to me."

170

"I just hope she doesn't give us a hard time. I really want to do this for her."

Her hand covered his. "I know."

"Actually, I've tried for years, but she always said no. I have a strong feeling she'll balk at it today, too."

Her smile was encouraging. "A lot's happened to her since the last time you tried to convince her. Maybe this time, she'll do it."

He squeezed her hand before letting it go. "I sure hope you're right."

"Don't know if I'm right, but I have a good feeling about it."

"I'm gonna take all these packs out to the Hummer."

"Okay."

"Hey, are you two almost finished sorting the mail in there?"

"Yes, Homer's putting all the legitimate mail into the Hummer now so he can pay your bills tomorrow," Carolyn told her.

"It's sure taking a long time."

"Just relax. Do you want me to bring the teapot out there?"

"Yes, that'd be nice, thanks."

Carolyn poured her tea, and then, she sat in the nearest wicker rocker for a few minutes, trying to slow her anxious heartbeat, as she sipped at her own.

"Thanks for the refill. Just tell me when you're ready. I'm having fun watching those baby chicks. They're so cute." She laughed and said, "Only in Key West would city people pass the time watching baby chickens peck the ground."

Carolyn laughed with her. "I'm sure you're right. Glad the city didn't get rid of all of them."

"They wanted to, and I don't see many of them around, anymore. I'm pretty sure this little family hid in our backyard when the bad guys were trapping them to take up the road."

"Oh, pretty smart of them to do that."

"It reminds me of the last time I spoke with Jackie," Maggie said, as she remembered . . .

~ ~ ~

171

"Hi Maggie, how's it going?"

She turned toward the voice and saw Jackie Weener sweeping the sidewalk in front of his haberdashery. "Oh, hi, Jackie. I'm fine. You doing okay this morning?"

"Sure," he said, standing with his chin on the broom handle as he stared at a little family of chickens who were walking toward them on the sidewalk.

"What's wrong? You look troubled over something."

He smiled at her. "Nothing's wrong, really, just thinking about last night's commission meeting and wishing they hadn't ruled against the chickens."

"Oh." She stared at the mother hen, who was trying to get her babies across the road before another car came by. "That upset me, too, my friend. The chickens were here long before most of those commissioners were born and although they can be little pests sometimes, I don't see any reason to take them all off the island."

"Nor do I," he said, with a big sigh, "but unfortunately, you and I didn't get a vote last night. Had I still been mayor, of course, I would have voted it down, but I lost that election, so it's a moot point now."

"Well, just for the record, had I had more than one vote, you'd be mayor again," she told him. You always voted with the people on every issue and you sure never failed to help me when I came to you with a problem."

That produced a wide smile on the sandy-haired former mayor's face. "Thanks, Maggie. You've made my day. Speaking of which, if I don't get opened up and ready for customers, I won't make a penny during it. Enjoy your day!" With that, he turned and went inside his store, as she continued up Duval toward her home. That was the last time she saw Jackie Weener alive, and it made her heart ache. She wished she'd never seen him after that in those dark mangroves . . .

TWENTY-SIX

"Mag, where'd you go?" Caroline asked.

"Oh, sorry, my mind just drifted to that last conversation with Jackie about the chickens. What were we saying before I lost track?"

"We were talking about the chickens hiding in the backyard."

"Oh yes, that's right. After being here for so many decades, maybe even hundreds of years, if the truth were known, I was glad to see some of them tucked away where they couldn't be found. I didn't want all of them leaving the island."

"I thought this family of them just came here recently."

"No, the rooster and his hen had been bringing their little family around late every evening for quite some time. They seemed to know what was going on, since they burrowed way back under that ficus tree until it was impossible to see them among all the roots and foliage. I watched them gather all the chicks back there, and then I didn't see them for a couple weeks after the roundup started. I put their food way back in there, when I saw what they'd done. It was always gone the next day." She smiled, and took another sip of her tea. "Oh well, I'd better finish. I'm holding us up."

"No, you're not, but I want to freshen up before we go."

Fifteen minutes later, Homer looked at Carolyn who'd just come back down the stairs. "I guess we'd better get this show on the road."

173

She bit her lip and touched his sleeve. In a low voice, she said, "Wait a minute before we call her in."

"Okay – what's going on?"

"It's just that – look, I know we'd planned to just take her and not say anything until we get there, but I'm having second thoughts."

"About taking her?"

"No, not about taking her, but about taking her and springing it on her after we get up there."

"Oh boy, I was afraid of this."

"I'm not saying not to take her at all, but I think as upset and sad as she's been over George's death, we can't just wait to tell her when we get to the office."

"Okay, I'll get her in here. You do most of the talking, though."

She smiled with relief. "Thanks, Homer."

When Maggie came into the dining room, Carolyn took her hand. "Let's go sit in the living room for a few minutes. There's something we want to tell you."

The other woman gave her a big toothless smile and then turned toward Homer and punched him in the shoulder. "Well, it's about damn time!"

"Huh?"

"You and Carolyn."

"What about us?"

"Isn't that what you wanted to tell me? That you're together?"

"Oh no, Mag, it has nothing to do with us."

Carolyn bit her lip again, and Homer put his hand on her shoulder and gave it a gentle squeeze of encouragement.

"No, this isn't about us. It's about you."

Confused, she said, "I don't understand." When neither of them said anything, awareness came into her eyes. "Oh no, you're taking me to see a shrink? Look, I told you I'd go into counseling if it continues for several months, but it's not really been very long. Has it?"

"No, it hasn't, Mag." Homer put his arm around her. "But, this isn't about your grieving."

"It isn't?" She looked up at him. "What's it about then? Has something bad happened again? Please, don't tell me this nightmare isn't over."

He took a deep breath, and let it out slowly. "Maggie, nothing bad has happened and it really is over. It's just that we - we've made an appointment in Big Pine."

"Big Pine? What's in – oh my God, you're taking me to see Dr. Troxel!"

"Yes, we are. I hope you're not upset with us."

Maggie stood. "Upset? No, I can't say what I'm feeling right now is upset."

Misunderstanding, Homer smiled with relief, as did Carolyn. He said, "You don't know how good that makes us feel. We want to do this for you so much. You deserve it after all you've gone through."

"Deserve it? No, I wouldn't say I deserve it." She was backing out the door, and they followed.

"Well, at least, you're coming with us. I'm glad you're not going to give us a hard time about it," Carolyn told her, as she grabbed her purse and followed them out to the porch.

"No, I'm not going to give you a hard time about it." She stopped at the railing and stood behind her red trike, looking out at the people passing on the street in front of the house. Before they realized what had happened, she had the combination lock undone and the chain off the trike.

"What are you doing? We're going in the Hummer," Homer told her.

Climbing on the trike, she smiled at him, "Maybe the two of you are, but I'm not."

"But, you . . ."

"After you give my apologies to that nice Dr. Troxel, go on to Key Largo and enjoy that dinner cruise. I hear it's pretty nice. I'll see you when you get back!"

She waved and then she rode the trike down the ramp on the other side of the porch, heading down United. They stood there, their mouths agape.

"Maggie? Maggie, come back, please!"

"Mag! Come back!"

"Maggie, let's talk about this!"

"Mag!"

"Maggie, please!"

Their frantic voices drifted away with the wind at her back. She made a right turn onto White Street and then left at the end of it to ride along the Atlantic Ocean. Now the wind was toward her and felt so good on her face. She smiled at everyone she passed, as she always had, not caring if they were shocked by her toothless mouth.

It was the first time she'd been on the trike since George Snow shot himself. Why hadn't she thought of it before now? This was her salvation. This was how she'd get over everything that happened on the water that day. It was what had been missing from her life, as she'd sat around moping about how she'd been unable to save his life. She wasn't going to let it be spoiled by those microchips, no matter how much Homer and Carolyn wanted her to have her smile back.

Sure, a mouth filled with white teeth when she looked into a mirror and smiled at people would be nice. But Maggie didn't need it. Not at the price of her freedom. She'd already been in jail once. She had no intention of going back again if something else happened and the durned ol' CIA found out because of microchips in her mouth.

The beautiful blue and green ocean waters were to her right. She inhaled the salty pungent aroma of it, and smiled at a man who'd turned from looking out to sea to greet her, as his small cocker spaniel frolicked at the end of its leash. The palm trees swayed and the gulls squealed. The silky Key West breezes kissed her face. In her sorrow over George's death, she'd almost forgotten how much she loved her island home, this old isle of bones. She smiled again, at no one this time. She was home and it didn't get any better than this for Bone Island Maggie.

ACKNOWLEDGMENTS

I would like to thank my youngest daughter Suzy Herne, hospice nurse and lover of Stephen King's and all other mystery writing, my sister Lela Buscemi, retired postmaster and fan of *Bone Island Maggie* from the first draft, Laura Smith, retired RN and friend for too many decades to count and supporter of my writing since day one, Tom Milone, activist and supporter of all Key West writers and who loves Maggie above all my other characters, Michael Haskins, Key West mystery writer and author of *Chasin' the Wind, Car Wash Blues* and other delightful Mad Mick Murphy novels, and Brooke Babineau, playwright and author of the exciting Key West mystery, *Below Mile Zero*, for being my first readers and encouraging me to finish writing about fictional, feisty 70-year-old Maggie Metronia of Key West. A special thank you goes out to Brooke, who also did a great first editing job on *Bone Island Maggie*, and whose suggestions were invaluable.

To those readers who believe the protagonist of *Bone Island Maggie* is this writer, that is preposterous and I vehemently deny any resemblance, except perhaps to once being 70 in Key West and owning a red trike at the time. But then, doesn't every 70 year old ride a red trike in Key West?

—Peg

ABOUT THE AUTHOR

Peg Gregory, a former Key Wester, lives in West Palm Beach, near her two daughters, three granddaughters and three great-grandchildren, two of them born within a month of her finishing this novel. Another granddaughter lives in Kansas. A retired RN, she is the author of Starfish, a romantic novel set in Key West and soon to be released in a revised edition. Her memoir, *And Then There Was One*, written under Peggy Butler, was recently re-released under a new publisher. She is currently at work on her next novel.

She likes to hear from her readers at **Pegb.gregory@yahoo.com** or through her website, **www.peggregory.com**.

Reviews are the lifeblood of authors and they are how other readers learn of them, so please review this book at www.amazon.com or at the website of the bookseller from which you purchased the paperback or eBook. If you must write a negative review, the author asks just one thing of you, please be kind. Thank you!

NewAtlantianLibrary.com or
AbsolutelyAmazingEbooks.com
or AA-eBooks.com

Thank you for reading. Please review this book. Reviews help others find Absolutely Amazing eBooks and inspire us to keep providing these marvelous tales.

If you would like to be put on our email list to receive updates on new releases, contests, and promotions, please go to AbsolutelyAmazingEbooks.com and sign up.

For sales, editorial information, subsidiary rights information
or a catalog, please write or phone or e-mail

The New Atlantian Library
Manhanset House
Shelter Island Hts., New York 11965, US
Tel: 212-427-7139
www.AbsolutelyAmazingEbooks.com
bricktower@aol.com
www.IngramContent.com

www.ingramcontent.com/pod-product-compliance
Lightning Source LLC
Chambersburg PA
CBHW030330020726
47493CB00004B/1213